Praise for Rhonda Parrish's Anthologies:

Sirens

"Poignant, diverse, and enthralling: this new volume in the Magical Menageries series evokes the majesty of sirens, from the traditional deep sea variety of Greek mythology to those that entice sailors of deep space to ones who scan modern dating sites with wistful hopes for a good match. I could not stop reading."

—Beth Cato, author of *The Clockwork Dagger*

Scarecrow

"Rhonda Parrish has assembled a stellar collection that runs the gamut of Urban Fantasy to Weird Fiction. Easily the most consistently satisfying anthology I've read in years."

— K.L. Young, Executive Editor, *Strange Aeons Magazine*

Fae

"These fairy stories are fully enmeshed in the struggles of today, with dangerous beings from under the hills taking stances against the exploitation of children and the oppression of women, yet offering bargains in exchange for their aid that those in desperate need had best think twice about accepting. There's no Disney-esque flutter and glitter to be found here — but there are chills and thrills aplenty."

— Mike Allen, author of *Unseaming* and editor of *Clockwork Phoenix*

Mrs. Claus

Not the Fairy Tale They Say

An Anthology

Edited by Rhonda Parrish

World Weaver Press

MRS. CLAUS

Published by World Weaver Press, LLC
Albuquerque, NM
www.WorldWeaverPress.com

Cover layout and design by Sarena Ulibarri.
Cover images used under license from Shutterstock.com.

First edition: November 2017
ISBN-13:978-0998702247

Also available as an ebook

CONTENTS

MORE WINTER STORIES FROM WWP

I'd like to dedicate this book, which is all about a strong woman, to one of the strongest women I know. Grammy, this one is for you.

MRS. CLAUS
NOT THE FAIRY TALE THEY SAY

INTRODUCTION
Rhonda Parrish

If you look up Santa Claus the top Google result is Wikipedia (because of course it is). Now, we all know that Wikipedia is a good place to begin research and a terrible place to end it, but it's perfect for the point I want to make, so stay with me.

In the opening section of the Wikipedia page for Santa Claus it talks about all the various names he's known by and then moves on to explain how he's known for bringing gifts to good children on Christmas Eve. From there it speaks of how the myth of Santa Claus began with a merging of a Greek bishop named Saint Nicholas, the Dutch figure of Sinterklaas and Britain's Father Christmas. Further, it talks about how he also has a lot in common with the Pagan god Wodan. The second paragraph about Santa talks about his physical appearance and how that has changed over the years. There is a final paragraph which offers more details about how Santa classifies kids as 'naughty' or 'nice', says *ho ho ho* a lot and lives with elves who make toys which he delivers with a magical sleigh and eight flying reindeer.

The opening section of Mrs. Claus' Wikipedia page, however, is a single paragraph. It says she's also known to go by 'Mother Christmas,' is the wife of Santa Claus (also known as Father

Christmas), mentions she's been referred to as Mary, Jessica, Layla and Martha and then includes one other sentence. That sentence?

"She is known for making cookies with the elves, caring for the reindeer, and preparing toys with her husband."

I discovered all this after watching an advertisement, of all things. In 2016, Marks & Spencer had a holiday ad all about Mrs. Claus. It showed her as a woman with a life independent of Santa. Like her husband, she helped children, but she did it with a totally different style than him. No reindeer or sleighs for her. No way. This Mrs. Claus rode a snowmobile and flew a helicopter!

I adored that portrayal of Mrs. Claus and it made me realise that I hadn't seen many portrayals of her at all and those I had were usually a rotund woman dressed like Granny (of Tweetie Bird & Granny fame). Then I started Googling and my disappointment grew.

I wanted to read stories about Mrs. Claus. Not tales where she merely makes cookies with the elves, cares for the reindeer and prepares toys with her husband, but stories where she is the star. Stories where she has agency, and personality and—like the Mrs. Claus from the Marks & Spencer ad—secrets from Santa. I had a difficult time finding those stories and so I decided to compile an anthology full of them. It's sort of like the anthologist version of the famous quote by Toni Morrison, "If there's a book that you want to read, but it hasn't been written yet, then you must write it."

This is that anthology. I'm excited about the myriad ways it portrays Mrs. Claus—a hero, a villain, a homebody, a spacefarer, an ass kicker, a motivator. It lets her step into the spotlight (sometimes alongside her husband, sometimes alone) and really begin to be more than *just* Santa's companion.

You may not approve of all the interpretations of Mrs. Claus contained within these pages, but I hope you'll find one or two (or more!) that really speak to you.

~Rhonda Parrish

WIGHT CHRISTMAS
Laura VanArendonk Baugh

It had been a long time since I'd attended the Council, so I suppose I should have anticipated that not everyone would recognize me. Still, I wasn't expecting to be challenged by a vampire bodyguard.

"Nobody gets close to the Skeleton King," he growled, putting an arm across the elevator door.

I didn't care if I were close to the Skeleton King—who, by the way, isn't a king at all, because Halloween isn't a kingdom and so doesn't have a monarch. He is, of course, a skeleton, but that hardly makes him special. But I did care that if I didn't take this elevator, I was going to be late.

I could have appealed to the dark-suited Skeleton King, standing in the back corner of the elevator with another vampire goon, but he was on his phone and I didn't want to bother him. Also, there's something to be said for taking care of your own problems, and I didn't want to appeal for permission to enter the elevator I'd been riding long before this vamp was undead.

I put a hand on his arm to gently but firmly lift it out of my way and started to step inside. The vampire twisted to plant a hand on my solar plexus and shoved hard. I stumbled back against the brick wall

3

opposite the elevator door, more surprised by the audacity than hurt by the attack itself. Vampire goon came after me, kicking over one of several trash cans lined up in the ill-lit alley. It was one of the old metal kind, and it clattered over the cement and spat refuse as its lid skittered free.

The movement and noise pulled the Skeleton King from his phone call, and while it's harder to read a face with no eyebrows, his posture definitely stiffened, even for a figure made entirely of bone. "Frank," he said, taking a step out of his corner. "I think you should—that is Mrs. Claus."

"Mrs. Claus?" Frank the vampire bodyguard didn't seem to get it. "What's she doing here? She's not the Big Man." He sneered, showing canines. "Go home and bake some cookies, Mrs. Claus. Maybe watch some *Cake Boss*."

I stomped on the upturned rim of the metal trash can lid, flipping it into the air, and caught the handle left-handed as it rotated toward me. I punched it solidly into his face and felt a satisfyingly solid connection.

"Shield boss, actually," I quipped, but he didn't catch my terrible pun because he was busy stumbling backward and trying to stay conscious.

The Skeleton King sighed (don't ask me how, paranormal biology is not my field of expertise, except the part about opening things up for easier examination) and made an excuse into the phone before hanging up. The second bodyguard was already protectively stepping between his employer and me, but the Skeleton King pushed past him to address the first. "Frank..."

But Frank's blood was up, or whatever you call it in vampires and, shaking off the pain and disorientation, he came at me with bared fangs and extended fingers hooked like talons. I swept his arms with a quick shield-circle which broke one of his wrists and then caught him under the chin with the heel of my right hand, lifting him from the cement as I stepped forward. I curled my fingers over his now-very-closed-mouth and threw him on his back.

"Wait—" tried the King.

But Frank wasn't the only one whose blood was up, and I was already in motion. I whirled the makeshift shield around and slammed the rim into Frank's face. They both dented.

"Sparkle *that*," I said. It wasn't my best line, and it was really just petty, but I was annoyed.

The Skeleton King's shoulders dropped. "It was his first week."

I tossed aside the misshapen trashcan lid and pointed at the damaged vampire. "He started it."

"He didn't know who you were."

"Maybe you should give your goons some sort of manual when you hire them, so they can read up on what they're supposed to be doing and who they might be dealing with. Then they won't walk up and pick a fight with a *valkyrja*." I looked at the second bodyguard, who seemed uncertain if he should be trying to intervene himself between me and his principal. "Yes," I said, "in case you didn't do any more homework than Frank, I'm a Valkyrie. Might want to remember that the next time you think about some sort of baking joke."

Second bodyguard glanced from me to his boss and then back at me, giving a quick, jerky nod.

"Great. Now that that's finished, can we share the elevator? Council meeting isn't going to wait on account of Frank."

The King gestured. "Step in."

We left Frank to his eventual recovery and rode up eighty-seven floors to the Council's meeting place, a long expensive table in a large expensive room surrounded by expensive windows overlooking an expensive view. It was like a board meeting for the very worst of Hollywood corporate villains, except that we weren't a board.

Or villains. Some of us have better publicity or methods than others, true, but all of us have the best of intentions.

I'm probably the iffiest of the lot, because I didn't come in for a good cause, but by marriage. This was already a bit odd, as few of the other Council members are married, and if you know anything about Valkyries, you know we're not exactly an embodiment of the Christmas spirit, but Nick had enough political clout and general accrued goodwill that no one made too much of a fuss about it.

You may have heard about Santa Claus having some attributes of the Norse god Odin, the beard and the flying and the frozen North address? He got those associations through me.

The table was mostly full when the Skeleton King—excuse me, Halloween—and I entered. I took a seat between Easter and Administrative Professionals' Day. When gathered, we are known by the holidays we represent, rather than by our own names. It saves confusion when times change and representative entities shift or are replaced. (The years of the Easter/Paschal controversy were particularly difficult.)

"Welcome, Christmas and Halloween," said this year's chair, National Tartan Day. He was nervous in his post, probably not accustomed to this much concentrated attention. He was one of the newer days of recognition rather than a proper holiday, admitted under our recent inclusion program. "Now we can begin."

I bided my time for the administrative trivia and general catching up on old business. It was about half an hour or so before we were ready for new business.

"Christmas, you have something to put forward?"

"I do, Mr. Chair. Someone is making war on Christmas."

The room went quiet and all focused on me.

National Tartan Day was not prepared to deal with new business of this magnitude. "What? War? How?"

"A dozen shipments of toys have been destroyed along western North America and several of our elves, riding along to monitor the cargo and confirm inventory at delivery, were injured or killed. There is no connection between these separate cargos except their designation as Christmas seasonal stock."

For a moment, no one spoke. Then several entities began speaking at once.

It had been a long while since we had been actively engaged in war. Many of our younger members had never seen it.

One voice rose above the others. "Do you have any evidence or are you just trying to get attention?"

Well, if today wasn't turning out to be a day for stretching patience... I gave National Raisin Day a flat look and said, "Do you really want to take this line?"

"I believe Christmas," Kwanzaa said in a warning tone. "This wouldn't be the first time. I don't remember those days, myself, but I've read the history."

"What happened?" persisted National Raisin Day. "Did someone put up an evergreen instead of a nativity scene?"

I was saved from answering by Kwanzaa's deep rumble. "Cromwell."

"Spit when you say that name," I said. "But let's not waste time on history. The most recent attack was last night."

"If this is so dire," asked Purim without accusation, "why are you here to speak as Christmas instead of your husband?"

"Nick is handling the recovery side of things," I answered. "He's better at organizing additional shifts, supply chains, updating the databases, making sure the children are taken care of. I'm better at dealing with conflict, taking names and running out of bubble gum."

"True," observed Halloween flatly.

"Ye have some sense t' what ye say, matey," came a new voice. "But 'tis a bold challenge ye be makin'. Do ye have any hint o' who might be plunderin' yer holds?"

I turned to answer Speak Like A Pirate Day. "Not specifically, no. But it's something more than mundane human work. Those shipments had elf escorts, as I mentioned, and they ended up injured or dead. Humans would have a hard time doing that with modern tools and practices, if they even notice them." Out of consideration I added, "Arr."

"How were they harmed?" This was from Halloween.

"Three were crushed as by a massive hammer, one is alive but unable to talk, another is wholly mad, giggling and incapable of rational speech. And one—one was eaten. We found his head and an arm, with visible signs of rending and gnawing."

Halloween looked as unhappy as a fleshless skull can look. "I too had some new business to report, and I fear it may be connected. We have lost some wights."

"What?" There were gasps or confusion from all around.

He held up a hand and began to explain. "In today's world, many of our creatures are extinct or endangered. Some can repopulate quickly, like vampires turning fresh recruits. Others reproduce slowly, and we have organized a conservation program with some success. One of our newer programs is concentrated on breeding and releasing young wights."

"And you've lost them?" asked Easter.

"There was a significant drop in our shepherd counts. I was going to request help in tracking them, if anyone could spare time or manpower."

"And you think some of them might have gone after our toys and elves?" I asked.

He raised and lowered his bony shoulders within his dark suit. "Those injuries are consistent with wight attacks. It's worth considering."

"Why would young wights steal toys?" asked Purim. "What would they want out of that?"

"The heart," Halloween answered heavily. "Wights often crave the emotion and trappings of human life. They want friendship, joy, love, the possessions born of wealth. Christmas is not a natural target, but it's an understandable one. They want the heart of the holiday."

I nodded. "I think I'd better see this breeding program."

❄

The Skeleton King and I took the low road to the hatchery. I wasn't sure entirely what to expect. For one thing, I found it hard to understand why we were deliberately breeding the things. I decided the best way to learn the answer was to ask the question. "Why are you breeding wights in today's world?"

"Predators are important," the King said. "They are critical to a natural balance. When humans drive foxes out of an area, the expanding rodent population spreads more disease to the humans. Predators keep worse things in check."

"Ah," I said. "And do dark supernatural predators keep disease in check?"

"Of a kind," the King said. "Say a group of young adults go camping in the woods. Let's say they are a jock concerned solely with his popularity, a girl who curries sexual favor by socially humiliating others such as the nerdy outcast tagging along in the hope of friendship, and a kind girl who finds unexpected strength in herself at the time of need. Monsters attack in the night. Who survives?"

"The kind girl, of course."

The King nodded. "And so humanity is culled of the least altruistic and the most unfit. Social disease is curtailed."

"But surely these predators kill some nice kids, too."

The King shrugged. "Barn cats kill songbirds as well, but you wouldn't give the grain over to mice just for that."

We emerged on a mountain ledge, looking over a long snow-covered slope interrupted at irregular intervals with mounds of various shapes and sizes. I had learned the sport long before it was a sport, merely a method of travel, so it took me a moment to recognize what I saw. "This is a ski run," I realized aloud. "Moguls. You're raising the little wights in moguls."

"A whole farm of tiny hills. It's perfect." The King grinned his ubiquitous grin at me. "Now, I'm going to call our shepherd, the one who oversees this brood of younglings. But you may wish to prepare yourself. He is not a young wight; he is an older thing and most find him... disturbing."

I gave him a grin of my own. "I used to weave fate out of the bloody intestines of men, using their skulls as loom weights. I am prepared to meet your shepherd."

The Skeleton King nodded and stamped his foot three times.

I felt it with some sense I couldn't name, an unsettling movement far beneath my feet like a shark swimming beneath a boat. I let one hand fall on my axe and turned to follow the sensation as it rippled through the earth.

He rose out of the ground as smoke rises out of flame, uncoiling to a full height almost certainly greater than it had been in life. His flesh was dark blue and faintly soft, as if it had considered rotting after death but decided against it. His hair was indigo and ratted into chunks, matted with dried gore.

The Skeleton King turned toward me, perhaps hoping for a reaction despite my brave assurance of a moment before. But if so, he was disappointed as I addressed the wight-shepherd. "You're not merely a wight, you're a *draugr*."

A *draugr* is an undead thing from my own world, a Norse man who did not fall down when he died and who did not stay quiet in his grave. They could be fearsome things, murdering folk or driving them mad, and they were better known for killing livestock than shepherding them. I wondered how this one had come to be given responsibility for the young wights.

His blue lips parted in an acknowledging smile and he gave a little mocking bow. "Indeed. You are not as ignorant as most humans."

That's because I wasn't human, but he would figure that out soon enough, and it would count more if I let him work it out himself. In his defense, I can pass more easily than an oversized blue undead warrior, but still, he had assumed.

"My lord," he was saying to the Skeleton King, "what brings you today? And why bring a human woman?"

The Skeleton King's bony expression somehow managed to look

pained, and I had the delightful idea that most of Halloween's staff were going to be sent through a couple hours of compulsory sensitivity training. "I came to introduce you," he said, gesturing between the *draugr* and me. "This is Lik. Lik, this is Mrs. Claus. She has some questions about the missing wights."

The *draugr* looked at me and did the math, and I saw *not human* register in his eyes. Good.

He gave me a small nod of acknowledgement and got on with the problem at hand, which was also good. "Have they made their way to the North Pole? That seems unlikely."

"I'm worried they made their way to several shipments of toys and killed some of our elves," I said.

That got his attention. He was old enough to remember the holiday wars. "I hope that's not the case. When did this happen?"

"The last one was two nights ago. An entire truck of donated toys for a domestic abuse shelter was overturned on the highway not twenty miles from here. The driver died in the accident, but my elves were taken out by something else." I reviewed the details of injury, madness, and death.

The *draugr* nodded. "That is unfortunate. And I am afraid I did notice some wights missing three days ago. They could have made their way to the city and found your truck."

"How are they getting out?"

"I don't know yet."

"How do we get them back?"

"How do you catch anything you don't want to chase down?" asked Lik. "A trap, obviously."

"Traps require bait."

The Skeleton King shifted. "You have toys. And lives."

"I'm not putting my elves at deliberate risk." *Ælfr* aren't anything like the ankle-high, ruddy-cheeked, delicate little flowers of standard North Pole art, but they aren't invulnerable either, and fighting off Halloween isn't in their job description.

Lik gave me a flat indigo glare. "Of course not, *valkyrja*. We go ourselves."

We sat on the framework of a giant crane, sleeping now after its daily work of stacking shipping containers. The position gave us a decent vantage of the docks and warehouse space below. Two shipments had gone wrong here, and we were keeping a particular eye on Warehouse 25, which held several hundred tons of dolls, cars, and whatever electronic beeping things were big this year. I don't keep up on this stuff; making kids happy is Nick's job. I make Nick happy. It's a good system.

Lik and I sat companionably in the dark, waiting. It wasn't awkward; I was a Valkyrie, a Chooser of the Slain, and he was the slain. We had more in common than you'd think.

"So, you were a *valkyrja*."

"*Am* a *valkyrja*. I just don't get called in to work as often these days."

"And you married Santa."

"Nicholas is what he goes by most often now. Yes."

"But Nicholas was a Christian bishop, at least for a span of years."

"Yes."

"Bishops…can't have wives. Or sex."

I nodded. "Frock-blocked."

Lik's explosive laughter boomed across the parking lot, shattering any pretense of concealment or stealth. He slapped his bare knee and threw his head back, laughing freely as any dead and drunk warrior in Valhöll.

A man crossing the parking lot below looked up at the sound of Lik's laughter, but it didn't concern him or disrupt his course toward the manager's hut. He wasn't someone who was afraid of being seen, then—but he didn't exactly belong here, either, not with a three-piece suit and expensive shoes that definitely did not have steel toe caps. The guy was a walking OSHA violation.

I nudged Lik and pointed him out. Lik frowned. "He doesn't walk like a thief."

"How does a thief walk?"

"It is hard to be specific, but generally not in a direct line across a well-lit and empty field."

"He's not afraid of any security cameras, I'll give you that. Let's find out why he's here."

We descended the crane and followed the man toward the hut, keeping more to the shadows than he bothered to do. He didn't notice. We were both Death, and humans so very rarely notice Death coming behind.

We arrived at the hut shortly after the customary greetings. An overweight foreman or manager was sitting back in his chair, trying hard to look dismissive. "I don't see why you people are involved."

"Workplace safety is very much our concern, Mr. Stephanos. There has been a series of serious accidents here. Falling containers are potentially lethal."

"You don't have to tell me the danger, but the point is, no one got hurt."

No one human, anyway. It's unlikely these men would have seen the injured elves, or understood what they saw. This was interesting news—if our elves had been struck by falling containers, that meant they had not been squeezed or sat upon by wights. And that opened the possibility that they had not been killed by wights.

Lik beside me was doing the same deductions and reaching the same conclusions. "Not my wights after all," he mused quietly.

"Let's find out why the containers fell," I answered, not yet willing to absolve Halloween completely.

The suit was asking about cleanup and complaining about lost time.

"Don't be ridiculous," answered Stephanos. "I'm not gonna pay a dozen men union wages to pick up broken plastic and circuit boards, not when I could put one guy on a front loader with a rigged brush and push it all off the dock in half an hour."

"You pushed it all—where?"

"What doesn't sink gets carried out pretty quickly by the currents here. It's a big ocean, no one's going to complain, and anyone who might can't track it back here."

Okay, if the possible *aelfr* murders might not have me on this guy's case, this did. It's not that the supernatural community is all ultra-green and tree-hugging by nature, but you have to realize many of us remember a time before the industrial revolution. We know what water tastes like without being filtered and chlorinated and fluoridated. We remember breathing truly clean air, something which no human today can say. And even more, we're going to have to live with this mess far longer than the humans making it.

So yeah, this guy was getting on my Naughty list real solid.

"Besides, you know how cheap that stuff really is before markup. It's easier to just report it damaged and get a new container. More sales for the manufacturer, more write-offs for the buyer, more hours for the workers, publicity on a shortage, prices go up, everybody wins. Money makes the world go 'round."

Well, if that wasn't the cheeriest of Christmas wishes. More sweatshop hours and an enlarged coastline for the continent of plastic.

Lik didn't have my personal take on Christmas cheer, but he was not any happier about this scenario. "I do not like this man."

I was about to answer when the desk phone rang, and I shut up to hear the foreman's half of the conversation. "Hello? Oh, yeah, yeah. No, we're doing fine, right on schedule, everything tickin'. Plenty of product for November sales, no worries."

A bang like a slamming door came from behind us, from one of the warehouses. I felt a rush of chagrin—we were supposed to be watching the toys!—and turned toward them. "We let ourselves be distracted!"

Lik was already moving too. The unshielded sodium security

lights were bright enough to eliminate the stars above, but through their glare we could grasp a hint of shadow near Warehouse 25. We ran toward it, silent in the night, silent like death.

Suddenly Lik flung an arm out to block my way. "Wait," he cautioned, stopping. "Wights."

He pointed and I could see them, about a dozen crouched together in the lee of the security light. The wights were about waist-high, and like all creatures were cuter as young than as grown things. These had large, luminous eyes and petite soil-colored limbs, and they looked like little twisted child-corpses instead of man-corpses. They were pushing something into their mouths with little snarls of protest.

"Rats," Lik said. "They won't like those. They're hungry, they'll eat them, but they won't be satisfied."

"Still, you could charge the docks for extermination services." I frowned. Did this mean my elves were killed by wights after all? It was true a few had come back mad, not injured; a falling container could not have done that, and that was classic wight work.

The little child-wights growled and shifted and looked down at the base of the building, where every few seconds a rat emerged and one of them pounced at it, snatching with malformed fingers and biting to subdue it.

"What stupid rats," I said, "to keep rushing out into predators."

There was the space of a couple of heartbeats, and then Lik and I looked at each other and started along the long wall of the warehouse until we came to a door. We leaned close to the gap where the door track met the wall and sniffed. Smoke.

"Why is there no alarm?" I wondered aloud, and then answered myself. "Why was there no safety chain on the fallen containers? These are no accidents—someone is destroying product!"

"I have to gather my wights," said Lik.

"I have to save these toys." I looked around and spotted a signal box. It took me only a few seconds to reach it, smash the protective covering, and yank the lever to start the fire alarm.

"No!"

At the end of the warehouse, pint-sized wights scattered beneath the blaring alarm, ducking away from the sound and scurrying in all directions. Lik turned from one disappearing shadow to another, unable to follow them all as they disappeared into the different patches of darkness.

Stephanos and the expensive suit ran from the trailer, shouting and raising their phones to dial.

Lik swore in an outdated language and plunged into darkness after the wights. A few minutes later he returned, still cursing. "Why did you scare them off like that?"

"I didn't mean to scare them, I meant to get help to stop the fire! That's why I'm here, to protect the toys!"

"I'm here to retrieve my wights! And you've just scattered them across the whole dock complex!"

Sirens began to grow in volume, drawing nearer.

Lik swore again. "We'll never find them in all this noise and commotion."

The morning news had the relevant details. "Gadget Mon School handheld games, this year's hottest holiday gift electronic, will be in shorter supply following a disastrous warehouse fire."

Not so disastrous—Lik and I had watched the firefighters arrive, had observed them combat and assess the fire, had stayed until the last trucks had departed and only the paperwork remained undone, and only a dozen containers were lost of the hundreds in the warehouse—but no newswriter ever held a job by reporting mild events.

Meanwhile, the effect was already rippling across the country. Prices of Gadget Mon School games had already climbed a couple of dollars on average, and pre-orders had jumped. Scarcity has a marvelous effect on desire.

Lik was still angry. "They were all there in one place! Just a few minutes, and I could have collected them!"

"You don't know that they were all in one place. You saw one group. Not the same thing. And a few minutes can make a huge difference in a fire. We needed to save those toys and make kids happy."

"Toys don't make kids happy," Lik snapped. "We celebrated a lot of *Juls* without your silly electronic machines. You know what makes kids happy? Not being eaten by wights."

I crossed my arms. "Is that likely?"

"Rats aren't their natural diet. They're going to look for something else—soon, if they haven't already."

I leveled a finger. "Your wights touch my kids, and—"

"Your kids?"

Inwardly I was taken aback. They weren't my kids, not literally or figuratively. Nick was the one who took care of the kids. But outwardly I showed nothing. "You know what I mean. Christmas doesn't look kindly on eating children. That's not what we're about."

"No," he agreed sourly. "Apparently you're about replacing expensive toys with more expensive toys."

Of course not, that wasn't Christmas at all. We—

Wait a minute.

I pulled my phone and thumbed to the maps app. "What will draw your wights? People working late, warehouses full of rats, anything to do with crossroads or travel?"

Lik, caught by my change in tone, frowned and answered seriously. "Crossroads don't matter to them, but the night workers and rats might. What are you thinking of?"

I found what I was looking for on the map, a perfect match. "If your wights are following my vandal, I know where they'll be tonight."

Gadget Mon School electronic games came in from overseas via the shipping containers and enormous freight ships and were brought to a trucking distribution center, where thousands of containers were unloaded and the cargo separated into semi-trucks to be driven hundreds or thousands of miles to waiting retail.

This was a logical place for another mass destruction of toys. But with a hundred loading docks and sprawling parking and truck lanes, it was going to be hard to find either. We prowled through the dark, our eyes and ears alert for both Lik's wights and signs of intrusion.

The air reeked of diesel fumes and cigarette smoke. An efficient locomotive can move a ton of freight over four hundred miles on a single gallon of fuel, but Americans do love their roads and trucks. Seems odd to me that anyone would add dozens of trucks to their morning traffic in order to avoid an occasional stop at a railroad crossing, but my rides are a flying horse and a sleigh pulled by magic reindeer, so I suppose I don't get a vote.

A man in a plaid shirt, suspenders, and work boots climbed down from a truck cab after backing it to a loading dock and made his way to a walk-door. As the door closed behind him, a black shadow moved in the wrong direction for the escaping light.

"There," I said, pointing. "That might be one of yours."

Lik turned in the direction I indicated and nodded.

"So, how do you get them back?"

"When I have them all in one place, I'll lead them home," he said. "Like a shepherd. But we need to find them all, first."

"You're just going to wait for them to show up?"

"I have a wight-whistle. They would come to that."

"Then why haven't you used it already?"

"Because they would come expecting food and ready to eat."

"And you don't happen to have any Wight Biscuits handy? Or would—oh. Oh."

Lik nodded. "Anyone in the way between them and the whistle would likely be killed. Since I don't know where they are, I don't know who would be at risk."

"Better sit on that idea for a while, then."

A man in a black t-shirt picturing oversized dice left a car parked well away from the trucks. Nothing troubled him before he reached an office door. Whatever wights were here, they weren't hungry or bold to the point of attacking adult humans. Yet.

He was inside only a few moments before a woman opened the door and held it for him to exit, now holding a stack of mildly dented board game boxes. "I just can't thank you enough," he said. "The kids at the ministry are going to love these."

The woman with him shrugged and waved her hand dismissively. "They're damaged, they're no good as product. Trash 'em or donate 'em, and who would throw away stuff that could be used somewhere? You're welcome to them."

"Again, thank you," said the man, balancing the games to shake her hand.

The woman went back inside, and the dice man started back to his car without a backward glance.

A tremor passed through the air, raising the hair on my neck and pushing my hand toward my axe. Beside me, Lik swore vehemently, angry instead of startled.

"What is that?" I asked him.

"A wight-whistle. Someone's calling my wights."

They came from the shadows, lurching up through the grassy dividers of the parking lot, and flooded over the man in the black shirt. The board games hit the ground and he collapsed on them, writhing beneath the swarm of ravenous wights.

"Do something!" I snapped, pulling my axe.

Lik caught my forearm. "There's nothing to be done."

"They're killing him!"

"No, they're eating him. He's already dead."

He was telling the truth—the man's spasmodic twitching was not his own, but the action of a dozen wights tearing at him from all angles.

I released my axe with an effort. "I thought you were a wight-shepherd."

"A shepherd, yes, but not their master. I cannot stop them from feeding once they've begun." He sounded a little regretful and a little defensive. And very angry. "But someone called them here, called them to that man. Someone is using them, perhaps even stole them from my keeping."

"Well, you said you needed them in one place to collect them," I growled. "There they are." And then I realized I had missed my own opportunity. "Who called them? Where is he?"

The wights had come up from everywhere, it seemed, but for the most part they had been farther into the parking lot than their victim. Lik had said they would attack anyone between them and the source of the call. That meant the whistler was in the building.

Goodwill, charity, and free product... My earlier suspicion grew stronger.

I turned back for the door.

I was halfway there when I noticed Lik beside me again. "I thought you were taking care of your wights," I said.

"They will finish feeding and then settle down in place," he said. "It will be easy to find them when I return. I can help you find your quarry as well."

"Thanks."

We slipped through the walk-door behind a woman exiting with cigarette pack already in hand and hurried across the open warehouse lane to the forest of stacked and waiting pallets. It was a glorious place for concealment, both for us and for any lurking malefactor, and I tried to listen over the steady background noise of whirring forklifts and talking workers.

I still wasn't certain of what we were looking for. This could be someone deliberately destroying holiday retail product, even freebies donated to charity, or it could be an ordinary vandalizing psychopath who had somehow happened to get control of some deadly supernatural predators. We couldn't draw conclusions just yet.

We went on, looking without knowing what we were looking for. We could hear workers calling greetings and instructions. Twice we stepped behind stacks of freight as forklifts whirred past.

But then we heard a new sound, a perilously off-key carol. "*They pay and exchange for loot not from a sled. Easy credit frees us, it goes to my head!*"

Lik and I looked at each other and dropped into predatory crouches, needing no words as we split apart to approach from two angles.

"*With cards running high and just minimums to pay, they'll owe quite a lot for many a day!*"

A figure sat cross-legged on a low pallet of dog food cans, a tablet balanced on his lap. "Two cents more each," he mused happily. "Doesn't seem like much but adds up fast. Three percent hike here, thank you! Lovely, lovely. The price must flow. It's going to be a big year—*gurlp!*"

This last was the sound of my hand catching his throat from behind, lifting him from his perch and swinging him around to bounce off a tall stack of cat litter boxes. He dropped to the concrete floor in a confused heap and looked up, eyes wide.

He wore a suit which would have been at home in any Wall Street boardroom but for its eccentric green tone and gold accents. Gold glittered everywhere, from his cufflinks to his tie tack to his watch to his teeth.

I stood over him. "Black Friday."

He grinned. "Using my Council name makes this Council business."

He's always been there, of course, but only recently did he achieve a day of recognition and so win a place at the Council.

"The Council already knows I'm looking for what's plaguing our toys," I said.

"I'm not plaguing them," he protested. "I'm making them more valuable. Those kids who would have been merely happy to receive a Gadget Mon School game are now going to be ecstatic, because as of today it's rare, a status symbol."

I snatched him off the ground by his very expensive silk collar. "Christmas isn't about status symbols!" I bounced him off the cat litter. "And those board games?"

He flinched as he hit the cat litter boxes but managed to grin at me anyway. "Those games were free. Not worth anything. Without them, people have to buy games for the needy kids. Encourages charity, you should be happy."

"You killed a man!"

"And now there can be a big toy drive in his memory, and the kids will get more games than just these donated few, maybe even a local corporate donation for free advertising, and everyone will feel so tragic and loving as they donate. All the warm fuzzies you Christmas lot want. You should be thanking me."

"Warm fuzzies?" I repeated. *"Warm fuzzies?"*

His grin faltered.

"Christmas is not about warm fuzzies," I snarled. "Christmas is about joy, about hope, about redemption. It's about peace, goodwill, forgiveness, and above all, it's about love, powerful love, incomprehensible love. Even those who do not celebrate the Christ Mass still remember these and respect them. Christmas gifts are not about status symbols or cost, they are about love." I leaned close to his worried eyes. "And you have made them about greed and death."

He rallied defensively. "You only want to criticize capitalism. Just another whiner who wants to feel morally superior to those who make their living possible."

"There's nothing wrong with capitalism until it starts destroying what you first wanted money to protect. Good business provides means to raise a family, build a community, preserve the land which feeds and nurtures us. It's commercialism which sacrifices family for work, exploits a community, poisons the land future generations need." I held his gaze and hardened my voice. "Which destroys the happiness of children, maybe starts a war."

"Don't do anything hasty." He grabbed for a golden whistle hanging from a gaudy chain about his neck and raised it to his lips. "I'll blow this and call the young wights from outside. They'll come to it and find all the workers in here. It'll be a Christmas massacre."

I rolled my eyes. "You won't do any such thing."

"Oh? Why wouldn't I?"

"For one thing, if you blow that whistle, the nearest wight to you would respond." I nodded to my left, where Lik was standing and listening.

Black Friday's vision had been filled with an angry *valkyrja* and he hadn't noticed Lik join us. His expression when he saw him now was quite satisfying.

"For another thing, if you blow that and set the wights on the workers here, you'll cause a massacre, as you said. Most humans won't know what caused it, but it will certainly grab their attention. That kind of workplace-related death, combined with last night's fire—and the container accidents which will certainly come out on investigation—will cause more investigations and safety checks and security protocols at shipping centers all over the country. Everything will slow down, costs will go up, and business will falter. Profits will drop."

I'd touched the nerve. I could see the war in his eyes, the desperate want to strike at me and the absolute horror of damaging commercial interest. He was trapped.

Lik frowned at him. "He's not so different from us," he said to me. "I fought for gold and wealth, when I was alive."

"You did," I agreed. "And you wore it proudly. And then your status was measured by how much you gave away to those who served you."

"Ring-giver." Lik nodded. "Yes, that is what we called our kings and chiefs. Coin-spiller. Breaker of hoards. You are right."

"And who is the greatest ring-giver? He who gives the most?" I grinned proudly.

Lik snorted, but nodded in acknowledgment. "Christmas."

Black Friday made a face of disgust, and I rattled him a little against the cat litter again.

"So, what do we do with him?" asked Lik.

I sighed. "Nick wouldn't want me to hurt him. Love and forgiveness and the spirit of the season and all that."

"Well, that's depressing," said Lik.

"I don't think so," piped Black Friday.

I turned back to Black Friday. "But Nick isn't here, is he?" I leaned close. "And you killed my elves."

I saw him realize for the first time that his shortcuts to commercial demand had opened blood feud with a *valkyrja*. "I—I—that was—"

I drew my axe and, with a short quick motion, swung it down into his foot. He screamed.

I waited a few seconds and then pulled my axe free, making him cry out again as blood ran out of his ostentatious shoe and into a pile of spilled litter on the floor. "You should be more careful in the future. You know how expensive workplace accidents can be."

He gritted his teeth. "We—we can work this out. Make a deal."

"Not everything is about the deal."

"For the kids. He would like that, right? Nicholas? He'd approve."

I considered. Yes, the little money-grubbing nose-dripping was right; Nick would probably want to settle this more peaceably and with some benefit to the kids. And no one wanted another holiday war. "All right, then. Let's talk."

And that is why you'll see that *cripplingly* deep-discount toy sale this holiday shopping season. You're welcome.

Lik led his satiated charges back to the mogul run and shooed them into their little hills as snow began to fall on the slope. I watched them disappear, not terribly sorry to see what I hoped was the last of them. I've got nothing against carnivorous supernatural creatures, but I prefer them older and able to carry on a conversation.

When they were all tucked safely into bed, Lik turned to me. "I still say you should have let me crush him and drink his blood," he said bluntly. "He'll make trouble in the future."

"Of course he will," I agreed. "But I can't take action for what he hasn't yet done. And I believe he'll be less destructive and more subtle the next time; we'll just have to keep an eye out for his work." I grinned. "And I do look forward to his next appearance at the Council. That should be interesting."

"Indeed." Lik extended an arm. "It was an unexpected pleasure to work with you."

"And with you," I answered. "Thank you for your help. I wish you a very Merry Christmas and a joyous *Jul*."

We shook hands as the snow drifted down around us. Then he sank into the ground, and I started back down the mountain, trying to pick up enough signal to flag an Uber ride. We still had a lot to do before Christmas.

THE ASYLUM MUSICALE
C.B. Calsing

December, 1853

I was standing in the yard when they brought her in, draped unconscious across the back of a wagon pulled by a morose mule. The wheels of the cart squeaked as it passed.

She wore a burgundy gown trimmed in ivory lace and a wreath of holly was tangled in her long, white locks. Her face, placid in her catatonia, did not betray her age, and her cheeks were rosy. I peered closely. Her ears were pointed at the tips. Odd.

I followed the cart a few paces, but one of the orderlies, Bruno, stopped me with a hand to my chest.

"Not now, Lizzie."

I retreated but couldn't take my eyes off the woman in the cart. "What happened?"

Bruno chuckled. "When we went to fetch her, we didn't know who to bring back. The farmer swore she fell from the sky. Can you imagine? Even showed us a hole in his cowshed's roof." He shook his head.

The baby kicked, and I rubbed it through the rough fabric of my hospital-issued coat. Bruno stared, licked his lips, and then turned to follow the cart.

Martha approached and leered at my belly. I did not like her. She'd killed her own baby years before, though she claimed it had been abducted by fairies. "Lizzie, who was that?"

I stared at the ground. "A new patient, I think."

Martha laughed. "Do you think she's the devil?"

My father had committed me for religious excitement. I shook my head and began to walk away. Martha taunted me with a song some of the other inmates had made up about me.

Lizzie Fields, she always sees
Demon spawn in you and me.
Lizzie Fields thinks God begat
Her mewling, reeking, worthless brat.

Tears welled, and I ran, both hands wrapped around my distended belly.

That night, singing filled the ladies' ward. I did not know the language, but the melody stirred something in me, a memory of long ago. I had been sitting near the fire on a frosty winter's night sipping apple cider hot off the stove. My mother hummed as she darned socks and the smell of roasted rabbit and turnips filled the air.

For the first time since my commitment, I slept as soundly as I once had beneath my father's roof.

In the morning, the newcomer was thrust into our dining room and left to fend for herself. The orderlies had replaced her dress with the standard gray frock we all wore, a sweater of similar hue over top. They'd cut her hair short, and she wore a cap to cover her head. She stood at the door, her chin up, surveying all of us as if inspecting a household staff. Were our aprons clean? Our frocks ironed?

Her gaze landed on me and slid down to my belly. The corner of her mouth raised a smidgen.

I took a deep breath, lowered a hand protectively to my stomach, and prayed. I did not like the way this woman looked at me.

Across the room, one of the patients began sobbing. I sat down to eat, ignoring the sound, but it continued to intensify. Many around me clapped their hands to their ears. Some began to rock. Others to croon in key to the wailing.

Martha screamed, both arms reached out toward the new patient, her hands clutched in rigid claws.

The newcomer, a stern expression on her face, approached Martha. She bent at the waist, whispered something in Martha's ear, and then brought their foreheads together.

Immediately the crying stopped.

A hush fell over the dining room.

The newcomer retrieved her bowl of porridge and started toward me. My heart beat quickly.

I glanced around, trying to find a way to escape. My breakfast sat untouched on the table. Bruno, who stood near the door, would not let me leave until I'd eaten.

Horror filled me as the woman approached. She seemed to expand, filling my vision. With each step, the specter grew: a maw full of needlelike teeth, sunken cheekbones, reptilian eyes. Her ears were pointed sharply, like a goblin's in a fairy tale book.

I squeezed my eyes shut and prayed.

A melodious voice, like bells and songbirds, broke through my prayers.

I opened my eyes.

The woman stood in front of me, poised and regal again, a beatific smile on her face. I didn't understand a word of what she said, but she touched her chest. "Yessica Klaus."

I did not want her to have my name. Names had power. But I could not stop myself from saying, "Lizzie Fields."

Lizzie Fields thinks God begat
Her mewling, reeking, worthless brat.

I couldn't say my own name without tears welling thanks to that cruel taunt.

Yessica Klaus sat across from the table, that beatific smile still on her face.

She touched the edge of my bowl, winked, tapped the side of her nose, and then tucked into her porridge.

I dug my spoon in and took a reluctant bite.

This was not the bland oat gruel we were normally served, but something altogether rare and special: spices, sweetmeats, sultanas, nuts. Flavors from my childhood filled my mouth. I savored every bite, reminded of the luscious holiday meal my mother prepared each year.

Wanting to share in this wonder with my neighbors, I glanced around, but none of them seemed as stricken as I was. Instead they all trudged through their meal, their faces as joyless and gray as the porridge on their spoons.

I looked across the table at Yessica. Only she seemed content with her lot, taking bite after bite in a repetitive manner, hardly pausing.

"You were the one singing last night," I said.

Yessica stopped eating for a moment but did not indicate that she understood me otherwise.

She did not need to confirm, for I knew it without a doubt.

Who was this woman, who spoke in tongues, sang like an angel, and transfigured porridge into a holiday feast?

Nor could I ignore the vision I'd had of her, as a screaming, ragged demon descending on me.

I emptied my bowl, stood without another word, and showed my dish to Bruno. He let me leave.

I needed my doctor.

He sat in his small office, making notes in his ledger.

I tapped on the door jamb with my knuckles. Dr. Brigham looked up and graced me with a tolerant smile.

"Ms. Fields, how are you doing? Did we have a meeting scheduled?"

"No, sir," I said, taking a step into the room. "Do you have a moment?"

"Of course." He closed his ledger and folded his hands over the cover.

I sat across the desk from him.

"I'd been doing better," I told him. "But there's a new woman, and I'm...seeing it again."

"The visions?" Dr. Brigham opened his ledger again, inked his pen, and looked at me expectantly.

"Ye—yes," I confessed.

"Angel or devil?"

"Devil," I said quietly. I'd often had visions of the heavenly and infernal hosts previous to my treatment, more often than not demons in the guise of my neighbors, my playmates, the congregation.

Those visions were one reason I'd been placed in the asylum.

The other reason...

I placed my hand on my belly.

"Are you feeling hysterical, Lizzie?" Dr. Brigham asked.

I shook my head. I could control this. Maybe I should have sought out the chaplain rather than the doctor.

"Good. You must remain calm for the baby, yes?"

I nodded.

"Would you like to talk about the father?" The doctor's standard line of questioning.

I shook my head.

"I think some time in the crib would be good for you," Dr. Brigham said. He made a note in his ledger. "Orderlies!"

"No, please."

"Yes, some rest in isolation will do wonders for your nerves."

I had not screamed. I'd caused no scene. The *spirit* had not come over me but still the orderlies entered, took me firmly by each arm, and led me to the Utica crib.

It crouched in a windowless room, a wooden cage raised on legs, about six feet long, two and a half feet wide, and twelve inches deep.

The orderlies helped me in as I wept. I dared not resist, for that would only make it worse.

I lay on my back, flat against the firm, unpadded surface. The orderlies lowered the lid.

My belly, too round in my last month of pregnancy, blocked it from closing entirely. The orderlies, however, seemed determined to make it work. They both pressed down. The bars dug into my stomach.

"Please. It hurts." Hysteria began to creep into my tone. "The baby…"

But they continued to maneuver, to prod, to work the cage's top down until finally they latched it. Then they left the room, one whistling a jaunty tune, and closed the door behind them.

I was alone.

My breathing refused to calm; some place of comfort in my mind eluded me.

Of course, I prayed.

I prayed and I prayed.

But no relief came.

The weight of the cage's top embraced us in an excruciating grip. I could not turn. I could not stretch. I could not move. I feared for my child.

Dizziness and nausea tormented me.

And finally I broke.

I prayed to God with all the fervor I could muster. I cried and screamed for help.

No one came.

Slowly my energy ebbed, and my voice became ragged.

Eventually—minutes or hours later, I did not know—sleep finally took me.

A sound coupled with a sensation woke me.

Thump, thump, thump.

Darkness surrounded me, but in the narrow, windowless room I expected little else. I tried to raise my head to look, but in the gloom, and in my weakened state, I learned nothing.

Thump, thump, thump.

Then I realized.

The baby.

Kicking against the bars.

Thump, thump, thump.

"Shush." I could just reach up to stroke the sides of my engorged belly, trying to calm the child within.

I crooned and prayed.

Thump, thump, thump.

Hinges squealed, and a tiny sliver of light cut into the room.

"Hel—hello?" I asked.

Footsteps crossed the tile floor, approaching the cage in which I was confined. I shifted my gaze as much as I could, trying to see, in the wan light, who approached.

The face appeared, and I screamed and shut my eyes. The white-haired woman, in the guise of the apparition which had descended on me in the dining hall, hovered above me. Fervent prayers ripped from me. I wanted nothing more than to be free of this cage.

A touch fell on my belly, soft and warm through the fabric of my shift, and then the beautiful strains of some strange lullaby drifted on the air.

The baby stopped kicking, and peace filled me.

When the orderlies finally released me and helped my limp, weak-legged body back to my room, I thanked them with my heart full of love and good cheer.

Christmas came. The director allowed the inmates to mount a musicale, and all fell to its production with zeal.

All except Martha.

She skulked around the fringes of the play, timid yet manic.

My baby would arrive any day, so I stayed away from the

excitement. Instead I read in the sunroom. The plants there were ill-tended, all on the verge of death.

Martha crept around me as well, as if she had something she needed to tell me but couldn't quite articulate and then one day she finally built up the constitution to unburden herself.

"The fairy took my baby," she told me. "Don't let her take yours too."

I looked up from my book. "I'm sorry?"

"That woman," Martha said, her voice barely above a whisper. "I know her. No mother forgets the demon who deprives her of her only joy." Martha's voice grew louder, her gestures more fervent. "She did it, all those many years ago. She did it."

"What?"

Martha kneeled at my feet and laid a hand on my knee. "It was winter. I'd gone out to gather kindling." She swallowed. "My birth pains came upon me. I was alone, miles from my home. And then *she* appeared, riding some giant horned beast. An elk, I think." Martha tapped the palm of her other hand against her temple as if trying to loosen something in her brain. "She helped me. She brought my baby into the world. I remember her hands: big, strong, knowing. The hands of a midwife. Then she sang us to sleep. *That voice.*" Martha stopped. Her eyes were watery. "When I awoke, the baby was gone. That woman had left me with—"

Behind Martha rose the imposing figure of Yessica Klaus, as if invoked by the story. Fear bloomed across Martha's face. Maybe she saw it in my eyes too.

Yessica reached down and clasped Martha's head between both of her big, strong hands. And, like that morning in the dining room, she lowered her forehead to Martha's. Martha's body went slack, and when Yessica released her, she slumped to the floor in a heap.

Yessica smiled at me, said something in that language I could not understand. With the words, reassurance filled me. She reached out and brushed my cheek and then turned to leave.

Orderlies entered, inspected Martha, and removed her from the room.

On the windowsill, the dead plants grew new leaves and burst into bloom.

The night before Christmas, the musicale took place.

The large hearth of our sitting room fireplace served as our backdrop, and those men best known for their manners and calm disposition were permitted to attend the evening's festivities. I was in no condition to turn a heel with the other ladies but I intended to watch.

Then the music began, and as the dancers took the stage, the first birth pains ripped through my womb.

I abandoned my chair near the hearth and, not wishing to draw attention to myself, retreated to the back of the hall. I did not know to what expect in this birth. No one had spoken to me about the bodily torment. My mother had shunned me and sent me here when the first quickening of my womb was apparent, and here…

Bruno stood nearby. I moved slowly toward him as cramps gripped me.

"Please, sir," I said.

But he only waved a hand at me and didn't bother to remove his focus from the musicale.

Another wave of terror and torture rolled through me. I could barely remain standing.

Then she was there, a grip like iron holding me up, murmuring softly to me in her incomprehensible language.

She led me to a bench and laid me down.

She crooned and tucked quilts about me. She held a glass of water to my lips, and I sipped gratefully.

Meanwhile, the women danced and the men leered.

I do not know how long I existed in that stupor of pain and expectation, but for all of it, Yessica Klaus kneeled near me.

When the baby finally made itself known, Yessica pulled and twisted and wrested it from me to give it to the world.

She held it up, a broad grin across her face.

"Is it a boy or a girl?" I asked.

She showed me.

I smiled. *A boy. The son of God.*

Yessica smiled too and handed him to me. I cradled the warm, slimy thing against my chest, wanting to be his entire world.

Yessica held up the umbilical cord in both hands, stretched taught like a tightrope in front of her, and bit through it. In that moment, I saw her other nature, that demon visage, but my scream died on my lips, for just as quickly, in the flickering firelight, the vision was gone and the kind woman returned.

She took the baby, wrapped him in her own sweater, and danced.

Exhausted, I pushed up on my elbows, watching her twirl away through the crowd. She showed the baby to the gathered inmates, parading him as if he were Jesus returned.

Which he very well might be.

Certainly not the son of a clerk at the mercantile.

Certainly not.

They kissed him and cooed over him, and I felt as if he was the star of the musicale.

Pride at having brought such a being into the world replenished my spirit.

Bells began to ring. I could not tell if the bells were from the musicale or the striking of the hour, but the peeling increased.

I glanced around, and a massive shadow shot across the windows, black against more blackness, long and narrow.

A commotion sounded on the roof above as if a coach and four had crashed. In the empty fireplace at the back of the hall, a rain of soot descended, dust puffing out as if the chimney had exhaled.

I swear, hooves struck the tiles on the roof. One after the other, like a herd of bulls pawing at the ground.

Yessica walked toward me, holding my boy, smiling, showing her rows and rows of pointed, wicked teeth.

Behind her, the women danced, the band played, and the inmates cheered and laughed.

My eyes closed as another wave of pain crashed over me.

Gravel tinkled down from the chimney, just audible over the show still going on. Then came a loud *thump*. Boot heels clicked on the tile floor. Somewhere nearby, Yessica spoke, her tone low and amused. My baby cried.

Someone replied to Yessica, a low rumbling laugh.

Unconsciousness claimed me.

I awoke the next morning, sore and unable to shake the visions I had the previous night. Surely none of what I'd witnessed was real.

I stood on shaking legs and gasped.

Someone had left a wondrous Christmas present: a cradle painted bright green and detailed with festoons of ribbons and clusters of roses, the work of a master craftsman. My hands clasped in joy, I approached.

Inside lay my perfect little baby. The boy smiled up at me, his mouth a perfect red arch as if stitched by God's own hand. Bright button eyes sparkled with silent laughter. He did not make a sound, no mewling or crying.

Such a good boy.

I picked him up, held him to my breast, and left the room. I wanted to share him with everyone.

I went to the dining room. I needed to thank Yessica for helping to bring my perfect boy into the world.

But I could not find her.

However, the other women of the ward swarmed around me, eager to meet the baby.

"Isn't he beautiful?" I asked. I pulled back the swaddling so they could see his precious face.

A few shrieks greeted me, but mostly laughter rang out.

Bruno sent the women back to their tables. "Where's your baby, Lizzie?"

"Right here." I showed him my boy.

Bruno shook his head sadly. "That's no baby. What have you done?" He kept shaking his head as he blew his whistle.

Martha ran up to me as I stood there, stunned. *What is happening?*

She grabbed me and shook me, hard. I tried to focus on her.

"She took your baby," Martha spat. "That fairy bitch. She stole him. I warned you."

"No." I held my bundle out to show her. "He's right here."

"It's a poppet, a nothing." A mix of disdain and sympathy laced Martha's words. "She takes your baby and she leaves you that doll."

From somewhere in her frock pockets, Martha produced a dirty rag doll with a perfect red bow of a mouth and black button eyes. She'd probably had it for a long time. I wrinkled my nose; lice crawled across its surface and moths had burrowed more holes in it than I could count.

She held it to my face. "Look."

"I see." I tried to retreat, to protect my precious boy from her.

"No, you don't see. Look!" She lunged for my baby. I screamed and pulled back but couldn't avoid her talons. She ripped my baby from my grasp.

"Give him back!" I reached for her, but as I nearly had my hands on my son, the orderlies attacked me from behind, wrenching both my arms behind me. "Let me go!" I shrieked. "Give me my son!"

The orderlies began pulling me out of the room.

I glared at Martha.

At the moth-eaten poppet she held up by one arm in her right hand.

And at my son, his bright button eyes sparkling with silent laughter, held up by one leg in her left hand.

Such a good, quiet boy.

DESPERATELY SEEKING SANTA
DJ Tyrer

From the outside, it didn't look like anything much, just another of the hills formed from glacial deposits that dotted the utter north. Perhaps, if you caught it at the right time of day, with the sun in the right position, you might see through the glamour that surrounded it and discover that the hill had windows and a door and chimneys, but that still wasn't the whole truth.

The hill held Santa's workshop, but the workshop was more than just that hummock. In fact, workshop was an understatement: Factory was more like it. Descending deep below the frozen earth, hidden from sight, the grotto was massive. It took the jolly elf that ran things a week to inspect every assembly line of the fifteen levels that composed the complex.

Santa was due back from his latest inspection. A woman in a white-fur-trimmed red dress and a little, wizened man clad in green were waiting for him.

"Where is he? Where is he?" The chief elf, Ruly, was pacing back-and-forth with all the gainliness of a duck. "It's not like the Old Father to be late like this; he's always punctual."

Old Father was the term of endearment the elves used for Santa, who was, literally, if some generations removed, the father of his people.

"It *is* concerning," said Mother Christmas, Santa's wife.

Although she kept her lips tightly pursed, inside she was churning with worry. She'd been married to her husband for 2000 years and only recalled one previous time he hadn't completed his rounds like clockwork, and that was when he'd picked up a spot of the Black Plague. (As an elf, he was immune to the worst effects, such as death.) Mother Christmas would never admit it, but if her husband was late, something was surely wrong.

"If he isn't back in the next three hours," said Ruly with a sigh, "he'll be late for the pulling of the big red lever and if he doesn't pull the lever on time... oh my! Oh my!"

She couldn't quite recall what the big red lever did—there were an awful lot of levers in assorted festive colours—but Mother Christmas did know that the pulling of each one at the appointed time, as well as the pressing of the various buttons and turning of dials, was essential. If her husband didn't pull it, there would be a delay and a delay could mean...

"We'll have to cancel Christmas!" Ruly waved his arms in agitation. "Oh, calamity!"

"I could pull the lever."

Ruly looked at her. "Old Mother, you know how much I respect you, but... *it just wouldn't do.*"

"But, it *would* be pulled."

"Yes—but, *you're not Father Christmas.*"

She rolled her eyes. It was impossible to tell if the younger elves were sexist or just couldn't comprehend anyone but her husband doing the job, no matter how simple.

"Well, in that case, I'd better go fetch him."

"Fetch him? Fetch him from where?"

"Wherever he is. If anyone can find him, it's me. Our hearts beat in unison and our minds are on the same wavelength."

Ruly gave a sniff. "It's a big place and we have just three hours till he's needed."

Mother Christmas smiled as if she felt confident. "I'll find him, Ruly, don't worry." Inside, she felt nauseous, but she wouldn't let it show. "I'll find him."

Fetching a red and white striped flashlight and a poker from beside the fire, she set out in search of her husband.

Even though all she was doing was giving each level a casual look, not the sort of detailed inspection her husband carried out, checking every cog, examining every toy and counting every candy cane, it was still going to take more than three hours to search everywhere: She needed to think where her husband was most likely to be.

He wasn't on the ground floor, she knew that; Ruly had been rushing about in a tizzy searching for him, certain he must be in the kitchen enjoying a glass of milk, or in his study sneaking a sherry. Based on his schedule and the fact no department on the lower levels had called to say he hadn't arrived, Santa should've been on his way back up. Knowing her husband, she was certain he would've returned via the sugar plum store, the candy cane depository and the chocolate liqueur distillery, so she would check those first.

"For you," proclaimed an elf thrusting a tray of sugar plums towards her as she entered the store. "Oh, sorry, you're not him. Your husband, I mean." He glanced down at the poker in her hand, then back at her. "Well, if you'd like one…"

She declined the offer. "So, he hasn't reached here, yet?"

"No, the Old Father has yet to arrive."

The story was the same at the depository and the distillery. It was worrying that he hadn't got this far. It wasn't like him to tarry when snacks were waiting—it was the promise of a tray of snapdragons that ensured he always completed the night's deliveries in record time.

She had to admit it: something was wrong.

Mother Christmas headed down to the next level and the production lines for dolls, dinosaurs and action figures. There was no sign of her husband.

"Begging your pardon, Old Mother," said the foreman, "but he hasn't been in to inspect us, yet."

It was the same when she visited the assembly lines for bikes, trikes, prams and peddle-cars.

"Sorry," said the foreman, "he hasn't been in, yet."

As she approached the train-set assembly area, she paused and sniffed. She sniffed again.

"Goblins…" The smell was unmistakable, musty like old leaves with a peculiar hint of cinnamon. They were like vermin around the grotto, endlessly fascinated with toys, which they invariably broke, and greedier even than Santa for sweet things. Vicious wars of extermination had been waged against them in centuries past, yet they remained.

Her grip tightened upon the poker. It seemed she had the answer to her husband's disappearance. With a grim expression, Mother Christmas began to search all the nearby storerooms.

"Aha!" Behind a pile of boxes containing miniature train buffers, which had been knocked askance, there was a hole smashed in the wall. The smell of goblin was strong here.

Goblins being of short stature, the hole was only three-feet high, but large enough to fit a rotund old man in with the barest of squeezes.

With a groan and the creak of joints two millennia old, Mother Christmas got down onto her hands and knees and crawled into the hole. Although not as rotund as her husband she wasn't exactly a svelte figure and the hole remained something of a tight fit to crawl into. Unlike the warm and homely atmosphere of the grotto, the tunnel was dank and chilly. Her breath, she noted, was fogging before her. Quite probably, the goblins had tunnelled in from some ice cave.

She sighed. She was doubtless making a mess of her dress.

The tunnel ran more-or-less straight for some distance before it began to head upward. It was quite a feat of construction; the goblins had probably been working at it for years.

Ahead of her, now, she could hear the raucous sound of a goblin party, most likely fuelled with stolen sherry and played upon pilfered toy instruments that were just perfect for their child-sized hands.

Slowly, careful to make no noise, she crawled forward. The tunnel began to widen and the ceiling rise a little higher. A goblin lay slumped in a niche, a bottle of iceberry wine clasped to its chest. It was snoring loudly.

Mother Christmas moved forward in a crouch, attempting not to wake it.

Suddenly, its red, rheumy eyes flickered open and it looked at her with an unfocused gaze. She froze. Then, it focused its eyes upon her and gave a grunt.

"Eh? Uh? What?" it exclaimed and began to rise.

With a deft swing of the poker, she knocked it back into unconsciousness before it could attack her or raise a commotion.

She continued to crawl along. Ahead of her, as she had expected, was an ice cave replete with icicles, its walls striated with intriguing patterns. Within were three-dozen goblins, or more, including a particularly tall example, a veritable giant at five feet in height. And, in their midst, trussed up like the proverbial festive turkey, lay her husband, his hooded coat torn from the struggle to bind him.

She crouched in the shadows and observed the scene, the goblins dancing upon his tummy, and tried to think of a distraction or other ruse to free him. Every inch of her felt the urge to rush forward and fight the goblins, but she knew she would have no chance.

Smoke them out? No, that wouldn't work; she had nothing to light a fire with. Once, her husband had always had a pipe in his mouth, but her success in imploring him to quit the disgusting habit meant he hadn't smoked in over a decade.

Scare them? Goblins could be stupid, but with no tools or tricks, the best she could do would be to cry "woo-woo" as if she were a ghost and she doubted they were *that* stupid.

Get help? That was the sensible option, although she couldn't be sure what they had planned for her husband. Probably, they intended to trade him for toys or to force him to make them gifts, but it seemed unlikely they would keep him here for long. Could she return with a contingent of elves in time? A cry from the large goblin told her she could not: "Come! Time to leave before they find our tunnel."

"Too late," she said and, not knowing what else to do, stepped forward.

The goblins all turned to look at her in surprise.

"What the—?" The big goblin leapt onto her husband's belly, which wobbled beneath his feet. Even through the gag, she heard the gasp of pain. "Mrs. Christmas... Mary..."

"Yes, that *is* my name—and, I've heard all the jokes."

"You cannot stop us... Indeed, you will make a handy extra prisoner... Seize her."

The goblins surged forwards in a confused mass, falling over one or another in their keenness to get at her. She hefted her poker and began to swing it back-and-forth as the goblins reached her, bowling them over and sending them tumbling into the icy walls of the cavern.

But some got to her and grabbed at her. When she paused to swat them off only allowed more to get near, grab hold of her.

Realising she soon would be overwhelmed, she did the only thing she could think of—she charged right through their ranks to reach their leader. One swing of the poker was enough to send it sprawling from atop her husband's belly.

"How dare you!" it yelled as it clambered to its feet and snarled at her, but she bopped it again and it slumped against the wall, dazed.

She paused to gasp in a series of chill breaths.

Behind her, the goblins had rallied from their surprise at being rushed and prepared to attack again. Even having bashed their leader senseless and knocked several down, they showed no sign of losing their nerve and remained numerous. There was an ache in her arm and she knew she couldn't swing much more. Soon, she'd be overwhelmed.

Dropping the poker, she seized hold of her husband.

"Sorry, dear," she whispered, then began to push him, rolling him like a barrel towards the goblins, a few managed to scatter, but mostly they were knocked down or bowled aside.

A moment later, they were at the tunnel entrance.

"Oi, stop her…" The big goblin's command was little more than a gasp; it still lay slumped against the cavern wall.

Mother Christmas looked about, but the goblins were either down, running away or standing about in dazed confusion. Only one or two looked ready to attack again—and those lost their nerve as they realised they no longer had the advantage of numbers.

There was, she knew, no time to pause to untie her husband—he could hardly crawl at any speed, anyway—so she began to push him, unceremoniously, along the tunnel, praying that he wouldn't become stuck.

There were no signs of pursuit and, at last, they neared the storeroom.

Suddenly, elvish hands seized them and pulled them free. She recognised Ruly, candy cane in hand as a club, at their head.

"We were just coming to your rescue," he said.

"Well, we're safe, but this tunnel needs blocking."

"I've got a fresh vat of glue," said one workelf. "Mix it with sawdust from the factory floors and pour it in and it should form a pretty good seal."

Mother Christmas nodded. "Do it. You elves stand guard till it's done. Now, Ruly, if you would, help me untie the Old Father."

"Certainly." He gave her a relieved smile. "Looks as if we'll be just on schedule. Christmas is saved."

Mother Christmas looked down at her husband. "Indeed, he is…"

CHRISTMAS MAGIC
Jennifer Lee Rossman

The air tingles with anticipation. Even humans who don't celebrate Christmas are celebrating the return of joy and hope and something resembling magic. All around the world, they watch the skies for the long-awaited visit of the big man in red, and their excitement is infectious.

Even I'm grinning as I stand in the doorway of the workshop, watching the elves load ton after ton of wrapped gifts into the hyperspace sack in the back of the sleigh.

Ugly old thing, that sleigh. I'd tried convincing Nick to trade it in for a sleek rocket-powered jet, but he insisted on keeping to some traditions. It was a hell of a job to fit the reindeer with antigravity reins that weren't too powerful (godspeed Dancer, first antlered astronaut), and for a tense few weeks it looked like we'd have to delay the ride when the lead deer's nose refused to stay lit.

But here we are. It's Christmas Eve and Nick's about to leave the North Pole for the first time in nearly a century. Presents are loaded, Nick has been prepped on the use of my shrink ray and cloaking devices, and Rudy's bioluminescent nostril alterations bathe the scene in a warm red glow.

Everything according to plan.

The rapid fire assault of flashbulbs turn my sincere smile into a practiced grin that does not extend to my eyes as I glare out at the photographers and reporters. I'm going to kill the elf who gave them access.

My husband, on the other hand, is nothing if not a people pleaser. He steps out into the snow, giving them the hearty "Ho ho ho!" they've been waiting for, all while posing with his hands on the big bowl of jiggling jelly that is his stomach. Then he walks over to me, and we fake our way through a kiss.

Affection is the one thing we haven't perfected. He didn't want to marry me, and I certainly didn't love the idea of wearing a frilly white apron and baking cookies all day for my old, *way* too jolly husband. And I could certainty do without paparazzi invading every second of my life and magazines scrutinizing every hairstyle and clothing choice.

"Who wore it better—Mrs. Claus or Princess Kate?" "Mrs. C. steps out in a hideous reindeer-skin jacket!" "Santa Baby Bump!?"

(For the record: I did, it was *faux* reindeer and that reporter wouldn't know fashion if it bit him in the jingle bells, and not a chance. Our species can't interbreed.)

But it had to be done and we've grown to like each other well enough, despite the staggering differences in age and personality. I think the public has bought it—the romance of it all—some days I think he has, too.

I play the part of the doting wife, seeing him safely to the sleigh, giving him a peck on the cheek to the delight of the cascading flashes, and wringing my hands as the reindeer pull him out of the workshop.

The merry sound of bells fills the air as they lift off. I stand in a sea of waving elves and clicking reporters, hardly breathing until the miniature sleigh and its eight tiny antigravity-equipped reindeer shrink into the seemingly endless night.

They're off.

I sigh, my body flooding with relief. Santa's airborne, spreading joy to a world long since deprived of magic. He's finally away from the North Pole.

I can't believe it's actually happening.

A voice recorder is shoved in my face. I push it away as politely as possible and make my way around the crowd. The elves act as buffers like they've been trained, but nevertheless one reporter finds a way through.

"Mrs. Claus," he calls out. I wince. "Could I have a word?"

"If you can keep up, I'll tell you whatever you want to know." I quicken my pace, ice and snow crunching under my boots as my brain churns for something to distract him. I guess I can suffer through one last interview. "And it's Belle, please!"

He falls into step beside me, a pale and wispy fellow with a face begging to be punched. His thin jacket can't be doing him much good in these winds that bite like a polar bear, but he isn't even shivering. Humans. So adaptable.

"Belle—" There's that damn recorder again. "—Earth has you to thank for the return of Christmas and, some would say, hope itself. When your pod crashed here just over a year ago, did you ever imagine you would have such an impact on the Earthen people?"

Aha. My pod! That'll distract him! I shift our trajectory toward the crash site, eyeing the glistening, striped pole in the distance. "In a way, yes," I say diplomatically, shoving my hands deep into the pockets of my red and white coat and longing for the eternal sunlight of Myra. "My planet has made technological advancements that Earth—and many other populated worlds—can only dream of."

We come to my pod, still half buried in the snow in the middle of the reindeer pasture. The weeks spent in that cramped metal tube were the most claustrophobic of my life, but it will be worth it in the end.

"We lived a prosperous life." Not exactly a lie, just not a very *recent* truth. "And our elders decided to share our wealth with the rest of the galaxy." That one is definitely a lie. "When I was chosen for the mission, I knew the technology and information I brought with me would vastly improve the lives of whatever planet I landed on. I just didn't know quite how."

I glance at the Pole, remembering how it used to glow with that unexplainable quality this planet called magic. I'll never forget that surge of excitement, all those years ago, when we saw it start to dim through our telescopes. A dying planet is a desperate planet.

The reporter follows my gaze, and I give him an explanation. "The magic in your North Pole used to power all of Earth. My planet is much smaller; even the residual spark of the Pole's magic could sustain Myra for decades. They would do anything for it."

That might be the most honest thing I've said since I landed.

"And the elves?" he presses. "Where did you find them?"

I don't blame him; for as much press as I've done, I haven't given many details. Afraid someone would piece together the truth, I guess.

"Ah, them." I don't have to fake the fond laughter here; I adore the little goofballs. "I understand you had similar creatures you called elves, when there was enough magic to sustain them. These are a species of mammal native to my planet's southern continent and comparable to your kangaroos, which we miniaturized through breeding programs. Very intelligent, with prehensile thumbs, huge litters, and a remarkably short gestation period. I brought one breeding pair and some cloning tech. A year later, we have three thousand." I pause and add with an eye roll, "The little outfits were Nick's idea, but it wasn't hard to teach them to sew. And they love the jingling shoes."

The lights appear in the sky, a line of tiny dots that extends from one horizon to another like Saturn's rings. My breath catches as two of the ships start to descend, and I avert my gaze so as not to draw the reporter's attention.

Hopefully the elves are herding the other reporters inside. I should do the same with him.

"Well," I say brightly, "the old man won't be back for hours. What say I get you an exclusive look at the workshop?" Hooking an arm around his shoulder, I don't give him a choice and steer him to the old barn. "Not where we make rocking horses and ragdolls—the *good* workshop, where we make the virtual reality goggles and the licensed fashion dolls."

I open the barn's heavy door, chattering away about how we make all the hoverboards using actual antigravity tech, and shove him in. I slam the door and secure the latch.

"Watch that one; he's trouble," I tell an elf, who gives a sickeningly adorable salute. "The others safely out of sight?"

The elf nods, miming drinking a cup of cocoa and eating cookies.

"The ones we dosed?"

It looks at me as if to say, "Do you think this is my first time drugging a roomful of reporters?" It definitely is, but I let the sarcastic look pass without comment.

Everything is falling into place, and I allow myself an excited little dance as I head toward the North Pole. Soon I'll be free of this icy hellscape.

The two lights in the sky grow larger, brighter. They encompass my entire field of vision, turning night to day as they spin and flash, their thrusters buffeting my hair and sending snow flying in all directions.

The crafts land, one on either side of the Pole. Beautiful ships, all sleek and curvy with a mirror finish. Their hatches open with a whispered hiss and their ramps extend to the ground.

My people come out in their suits of silver and gold. Funny; I never noticed how silly we look in those things.

Oh, stars. Have I actually grown fond of my furry red getup and its stupid apron, with its delicate embroidered flowers and—admittedly kind of cute—lace details?

Gross.

I welcome the Myrans with our traditional, impersonal arm touch, and smile at the thought of how they would react if I hugged them. It's going to take a while to rid myself of these disgusting Earth customs.

It's clear by their expressions that the dimly glowing Pole does not impress them.

"It might not look like much," I say, caressing the warm, striped pillar, "but the scant magic it still has is giving life to the entire planet. And it's a bigger planet than ours, with billions of people and animals—"

"Earthlings," corrects one of the Myrans, "are not people."

The other nods, holding up the extraction device that will pull all the energy from deep within the planet. "To be back home when it happens," he says with a wistful sigh, "watching as the lights blink out."

A grin spreads across the other's face. "One by one by one, until the planet's dark and dead!"

I cross my arms but say nothing, turning away as they start to tap the Pole like it's a maple tree.

I'm going to miss maple syrup. Pancakes. We don't have anything as sweet back home, but maybe with our magic up and running again, we'll be able to whip up a facsimile.

The barn door rattles. Mr. Reporter Man trying to break out. I can't help but smile; so resilient, the humans. Cute, too, with their fuzzy heads and skin that comes in such a variety of nice brown colors. I like my green skin—very Christmassy against my red outfit—but their colors are so rich and beautiful.

It's a shame, really. These humans...I don't think they'll survive more than a few hours without their magic, even with the advancements in technology I've given them.

What good are antigravity reindeer when you're dying from the radiation a strong magical field helps suppress?

The high-pitched whirring of the drill grates on my ears, but I still hear the rattling door.

Why did it have to be Earth? None of the other planets we've harvested were so welcoming. What twist of chance had me land here instead of on some world populated by murderous squid people?

Poor little humans.

A satisfied gasp behind me, and the drill cuts out. They've reached the core.

I glance over my shoulder. The magic flowing into their container is more beautiful than I ever imagined, a black liquid that shines from within itself, light escaping in a million tiny pinpricks. It's a universe in a jar.

"You looked pained," the female says. "What's wrong with you?"

"Does the imminent death of a world not bring you joy?" the male adds.

As much as it disturbs me to admit, I think my silence is answer enough.

Wait. Silence?

The barn door has stopped rattling. I storm over to it and see the reporter watching through a knothole in the wood, his face aglow with the blue light of his phone.

His eyes light up when he sees me. "Belle. Thank god. Those things are stealing—"

"Things?" I repeat coolly, trying not to care. Trying to stay loyal to the mission. "I believe you're referring to my people."

This information sends him into outrage. "Your people? You're from a peaceful planet! Why are they—"

"I lied."

The phone still glows in his hands. The website he works for will want an exclusive, but I don't believe he's that stupid or selfish to be contacting them. When you see aliens attacking your planet, you don't call the media. You call for help.

"Belsnickel!" one of the Myrans calls out. My horrible real name. It means stealer of hope. "What are you doing?"

"Who are you calling?" I demand, ignoring her.

I think I scared the poor man. He drops his phone, backing away from the door. "Was it all a big scam?" he whispers.

"Who are you calling?" I ask again, but his attention is pulled toward something behind me. I turn, and there's my answer.

A little red light in the sky, the kind made by a reindeer with augmented nasal passages.

Nick.

He sent out some kind of distress signal and called Nick back.

The Myrans notice it, too. "No problem," the male says, lifting a pulse gun skyward. One shot and Nick will be dead, plummeting into the icy Arctic Sea.

I try so hard not to care. I don't love Nick, or his perpetual jolly attitude. His laughter irritates me, and I truly despise the idea of being the wife of an elderly toymaker in this frozen wasteland of infinite merriment.

But I think I really care about him.

He took me in before he even knew my tech could help him, when I was just a crashed alien girl with fangs and green skin. It was almost too easy to dupe him, because he's just so damn sweet and trusting.

They all are, the humans. A hopeful little species that knows most of the galaxy wants to kill them and strip their planet of its resources, but that still looks up at the night sky and says, "Maybe the next ones will be friendly."

The magic is all drained from the Pole, leaving it dark and lifeless, but still the planet lives, its skies dancing with color. I think the real magic might come from its people.

And that's why I do something really stupid.

Without a thought to my own safety or the wellbeing of the people of Myra, I leap onto the Myran with the pulse gun. We crash to the ground, snow blasting up as he pulls the trigger, missing me by inches.

Before I can fully grasp what I'm doing, I yank the pulser away and fire it at the Myrans.

There's no sound, no blood. They just fall down dead.

I drop the gun and grab the jar of swirling magic, hugging it to myself. And I stand there, numb and cold despite my furry coat, while the elves swarm around in a confused frenzy.

Only when the sleigh lands do I snap back to my senses.

An arm goes around my shoulder, pulling me close. A beard tickles the side of my face.

"What happened, Belle?" It isn't an accusation. There's no suspicion or anger in his voice.

Stupid humans and their trust. Does he not see the magic in my hands? The gun and dead Myrans at my feet? How can he look at me and see anything but a monster come to steal his planet's life?

"What happened?" he asks again.

"I don't really know," I say. I don't want to lie, not to him, but the truth starts with my admitting that nothing he knows about me is true and I don't want to hurt him because...

Because I want him to let me stay.

I speak fast so he can't interrupt, and the words tumble out of my mouth. "We came for your magic. Our planet is dying, so we steal life from other planets. My pod didn't crash; I landed it here so I could earn your trust and help you make your flight. Not to bring Christmas back to the world but just to get you out of the way so the Pole would be defenseless."

I gesture to the dead Myrans. "I killed them. To protect you. But more are coming and I'm so sorry and—" I blink quickly to dry the tears that will freeze on my face. "And there's a reporter locked in the old toy factory, and a lot of sedated ones in the house. Don't drink anything the elves give you."

Nick looks at me for a long moment, then laughs that hearty laugh of his. I only realize there was a knot in my stomach as it slowly unties itself. He doesn't hate me.

"Well, I don't approve of the reason it happened, but myself and the planet are forever in your debt." He takes the jar and examines it through his half-moon glasses. "That's more than enough to share. So, first we'll send a scientist up to Myra with a sample of the magic. Human ingenuity and Myran tech; we'll see if they can't work together to replicate it."

The lights of the reinforcements are already growing brighter in the sky.

"Belle, my dear," he says, squeezing my shoulders as he guides me towards the barn, "do you know why they would only attack when I was away?"

I shake my head, and Nick presses a button on a handheld device he pulls from his pocket. The roof of the reindeer barn opens, gears creaking in protest.

"Because I have an enormous laser beam."

Okay, so maybe this planet is a little bit awesome.

GOOD MORNING
Kristen Lee

Eve had always been an early riser. In her old life, this meant awakening in the still, quiet dark, before even the birds dared lift their heads from the warmth beneath their wings. She'd stoke the hearth, set the day's bread to rise, and feed the dogs. Chores done, she would take her breakfast to the ridge behind her house, shadowed by the most loyal canines, and dangle her feet over the edge as the sun rose.

The brilliance of her memory has faded over the years. Centuries later, the colors of the sunrise in her dreams appear dull, tinted blue, blurry around the edges. But in her old life, the first kiss of the sun as it broke the horizon had been more than enough to rouse her from the warmth of her bed into the pre-dawn chill.

Now, wakening is a slow process. The breaking of the spell starts in her fingers and creeps through her veins. Her dreams muddle as the thaw spreads, and there's always a brief, glorious second during which she believes she will open her eyes to the soft glow of a newborn sun.

Instead, Eve is greeted by the navy-dark of the North Pole. Even the faerie fires that illuminate the chamber blaze with the cold, blue light of stars. Their glow—though relatively dim—burns her eyes, and tiny replicas flash behind her closed eyelids. Her vision adjusts before her body remembers how to move, and as her blood rekindles, she watches the slumbering form of her husband.

Nick is still confined within the crystalline ice. The uneven facets warp his glamour, so he flickers young-and-beautiful and old-and-jolly all at once. Beneath his age-whitened hair are Nick's black curls; beneath his cloud of beard, the squared-off jawline Eve had pressed countless kisses to before their lives became bound to December 25th. Even frozen, his long-lashed eyes flit in dream beneath his lids. She wonders if he dreams of her.

Misty breath gusts over Eve's hand. In her frigid state, the ghostly warmth burns, and she twists to escape the pain. Hooves clatter against the icy floor of the chamber, and Eve draws herself painfully upward to see Dancer—her favorite of the reindeer—staring dolefully at her. She wants to reassure the beast, but her lips are cold-cracked and her tongue frozen to her teeth. Instead, she raises her stiff arm, and Dancer sheepishly creeps back over to rub her shaggy head against Eve's outstretched hand.

Eve loves the reindeer, but in moments like this, she misses the dogs. She yearns for their ever-wagging tails and their soft-tongued kisses. She misses their love of running so strong that it twitches their legs in their sleep. She misses the dogs and the rising sun and holding Nick, *talking* to him, and—

Dancer butts her head against Eve's palm as though to remind her that here, too, chores must be completed. Holding the deer for support, Eve rises on shaky legs. Together, they shuffle their way to the makeshift kitchen—a counter, a cook stove, a table, two chairs—all cobbled together from scrap wood and rough stone.

Laid out atop the counter are the ingredients for the daily bread. Eve is never entirely sure how they get there, though she suspects the elves since they run everything else here. There's something ethereal about the ingredients—the snow white flour too fine to have been ground from common wheat, the crystals of sugar as individual as snowflakes, the oil faintly glowing—but in the face of her hunger, things like where and how become matters of least concern.

What does concern Eve is how much harder it is to knead the dough this year. Perhaps sleeping encased in ice for so long has led to muscle atrophy. Or, perhaps, the interminable amount of magic it takes to successfully pull off Christmas Day is finally taking a toll on her pitifully human form. Neither option is particularly attractive.

While the bread bakes over the faerie fire, Eve pets Dancer, reveling in the soft warmth of her solid body. Her fur always reminds Eve of tarnished silver. Like everything here—snow, ice, water, sky of endless night—she lacks color beyond the dull, cool, or neutral. Eve misses vibrance and hue. Eve misses the sun.

The bread is cooling on the table when footsteps startle her out of a half-doze. Dancer has wandered off—likely at the beck of the elves—leaving Eve alone with her recently wakened husband. Even after centuries, there's a moment of startle at seeing Nick in full glamour. Her eyes latch hungrily to the ripe cherry velvet of his suit, to the strawberry blush brushed across his cheeks and nose.

"Good morning," Eve whispers, her voice ravaged by a year's disuse.

Nick grunts an acknowledgement. As he brushes past Eve to his waiting chair, he presses a kiss to her chilled forehead that lingers for one brief, brilliant moment like a ray of sunshine. When he breaks the bread and presents her with the noticeably larger half, neither mentions it. They eat in silence.

Just as Eve is thinking that maybe this is the year she asks Nick what he dreamt, he pushes away from the table, chair legs groaning, and leaves the chamber to begin his preparations. With a sigh, Eve licks the crumbs from her fingers and exits from the opposite direction to begin her own.

The cleansing is the worst part. Each year, Eve forces herself to strip out of her simple linen shift and rub cinnamon-scented oil into skin soft from hibernation. She lingers, coating her shoulders, cheeks, and legs until every drop from the vial has been spent. Then, unable to postpone any longer, she walks to the edge of the ice.

Every year, the plunge rips the breath from Eve's lungs. Enveloped beneath the cold, dark waves, she doesn't know which way is up. Precious air rushes away in bubbles that she thinks might've been beautiful in another life. Her heart hammers with the fear that this is the year the currents pull her into the infinite void of the ocean's depths. But, inevitably, she surfaces, gasping and spitting salt water and very much alive.

Back on solid ice, Eve dries herself before donning the ceremonial robe. The brocade silk shimmers a million hues—all of them blue. She runs her fingers gently over the raised silver embroidery—runes, old symbols of power, whose true names she's forgotten like the vibrant colors of sunrise. This one *endurance*, and that one *patience* or... no, *courage*. Cheeks burning in shame, she cinches the robe closed with its equally lavish sash.

The time has not yet come to begin the incantation, so Eve plaits her hair for no reason other than Nick once said—a long, *long* time ago—that that was the way he liked it best. It had been braided when they first met—Eve and her dogs emerging from the woods just as the weary, lost traveler was about to give up hope and turn back the way he'd come—and she likes to think that it's for sentimental reasons rather than cosmetic that he prefers it as such.

Sentiment is, after all, why Eve had given his glamour a red suit— her small mark of rebellion against the elves. She'd balked at first, when they insisted she create a false appearance for Nick, one that would evoke the magical joy of Christmas rather than the fear of a commoner stealing by night into their houses. In the end, selfishness had broken her down—she wanted to keep a thin sliver of her husband to herself, and if it was his appearance, then so be it. The elves had seemed pleased, or at least stopped harrying her once it was done.

What the elves didn't know was that the crimson velvet was to evoke the roses Nick had brought to her house when he'd tracked her down nearly three months later. As she ties off her braid, she wonders if the roses, carefully pressed between the thin pages of a heavy book, still exist somewhere beyond the Pole or if they've since turned to dust.

The elves call with silver bells, and Eve takes just a moment to adjust her robe before heeding them. Glamoured-Nick is already there, settled atop his sleigh, and the harnessed reindeer paw impatiently at the icy ground. Before them, a blaze of faerie fire gnaws at a pile of offerings: crayon scribbled pictures, parent-inked letters, millions upon millions of cookies.

Eve pats the friendlier reindeer as she passes them on her way to the sleigh where she stands on the raised bed to kiss Nick's cheek. "Safe journey," she murmurs. He clasps her hand in his, the warmth of his skin seeping through the white gloves of his glamour.

"Good night, love," he replies.

Eve swallows and nods. She draws a symbol of protection on his forehead with her index finger before circling the sleigh and reindeer while weaving a spell of exclusion around them. She ties off the thread of magic with a neat bow before taking a deep breath to steady herself for the night's true magic.

Eve makes her way to the fire. She walks around it in a perfect circle, then traces her footprints in the opposite direction. When she's pleased with the quality of her work, she retrieves a silver pail of ocean water. She paces her circle once more, slowly, sprinkling the water as she recites the incantation so ingrained in the fabric of her being that she's certain she'd sooner forget her own name. As the water hits the ice, it sizzles and glows.

As soon as the circle is complete, the fire extinguishes with a loud hiss, a wind whipping outwards that threatens to tear Eve's braid loose. The world darkens as the gale passes over it, leaving only the dull silence of frozen time. Eve has to force herself to breathe the still air—in, out, in, out—as the magic floods out of her.

The ashes crackle and begin to glow, not with faerie fire but with the aqua light of Eve's magic. They rise into the air, almost tentatively at first, then spiraling upward in droves, forming a perfectly round disc decorated with organized fractal chaos. As the final pieces fly into place, Eve feels her blood enflame within her veins. There's a blinding blaze of light, and the portal is complete.

Exhilarated, the reindeer race toward the portal and launch themselves through, taking Nick with them and leaving Eve alone on the North Pole but for the elves who hide on the fringes and work only in secret. It always feels like seconds and eons at once as she waits for her husband's return, for the brief glimpse of his face before the exhaustion hits and she collapses. Nick's own magic is minute in comparison, but it's enough to keep them safe as they slumber until the next Christmas.

Sometimes in her dreams, Eve sees Nick carrying her to their bed and laying her gently across it, before exchanging the heavy ceremonial robe for her age-soft sleep shift. He kisses her knuckles, unbraids her hair, and as he makes his final preparations, he tells her about riding the space fractals through the still world—snowflakes frozen in mid-air, coils of smoke hanging above chimneys, glittering metal vehicles with magic lights of their own. She likes to think he holds her hand as the spell takes over and the ice envelopes them, but she's never sure how much of what she dreams is true.

Eve is shaking and her vision flickers in and out. She knows it won't be long now before Nick emerges from the portal, but not-long in a timeless space still feels like an eternity. She wants to tell Nick to hurry, but even if by some miracle he could hear her, speaking would shatter the spell and leave him stranded in the unknown between time and space.

Eve feels Nick's arrival before she sees him—a sharp shuddering in her bones. As he passes through the portal, a luminous flare backlights him, cutting through his glamour. But it's not his true form she is captivated by; rather, it's the warm brilliance of echoed sunlight. It's gone in an instant, but sunspots dance in her vision and she *wants*—more than anything—to be wherever he came from, the land not held hostage by the dark and cold.

Before Eve realizes what she's doing, she's taken an unsteady step towards the memory of sunshine. Then another, and another, and her legs must forget they can barely support her weight, and she's running, racing towards the portal.

"*Eve!*"

Eve leaps into the portal. Nick's desperate scream rings in her ears as the North Pole fades to nothingness.

Minutes, hours, an eternity later, Eve wakes to the soft kiss of snowflakes brushing against her face, clinging to her eyelashes. Her bones ache, crackling with the frayed remnants of her magic. Her skin is tender, especially around the joints. Her robe is in tatters, imprints of the embroidered runes singed into her flesh.

The salt and shift of the sea is gone. Eve smells earth beneath the snow, muted and frozen, and can barely make out the dark outlines of trees in the dark. She's not sure where or even when she landed, but a giddy smile graces her face—she's escaped.

The desire to sleep for a year weighs heavy upon Eve, but she battles it and forces herself onto unsteady legs. She's surrounded by trees, and after risking her life for one more sunrise, she'll be damned if she lets anything obstruct her view.

By the time Eve stumbles out of the woods, the sky has lightened to the soft silver of Dancer's pelt. A lone bird warbles a song in the thicket behind her, and something small and quick—a squirrel, maybe a rabbit—darts into the winter-dead field before her.

A few paces away, a lone bench waits, and Eve sinks gratefully onto it. The eastward sky grows brighter, a pink along the horizon so faint she thinks perhaps it's an illusion born of memory and anticipation. Nothing could tear her eyes from the sunrise. Nothing but—

"*Eve!*"

The battered figure emerging from the forest calls her name again as he staggers towards her. Nick half-collapses onto the opposite end of the bench. His glamour is gone without Eve's magic to steady it, and his skin is etched with thin lines of blood that branch like ice crystals. Eve longs to trace them with her fingertips, soothe them, heal them, but her husband's anger is palpable. She turns her gaze back to the sky.

"Did you think…" Nick takes a deep breath that does nothing to stay the tremble in his voice. "Did you *think* before you jumped?"

Eve hadn't, not really, but this knowledge will grant him no peace of mind, so she stays silent.

"You could've ended up anywhere all alone, and y—no. No! Worse. You could've died. You could've destroyed the fabric of time and space." Nick seethes; the clouds bleed pale peach. "What's going to happen to Christmas?"

The thought of Christmases to come hadn't so much as crossed Eve's mind. She wants to comfort him, to tell him that the elves, crafty and mysterious as they are, will beguile some other poor innocents into their vacant roles with glittering promises of immortality and fame. But before she can open her mouth, the sun peeks over the horizon and unfurls rosy fingers, taking her breath away completely.

Later, Nick will tell Eve how the reindeer screamed, how the elves had dared peer out of their hidden places. He'll whisper about the fear that stopped his heart, and the terror that spurred him toward the portal, which had begun to unravel without her magic binding it together. He'll recount his hard landing on solid, unknown ground and the miles he'd wandered until, by some small miracle, he'd found her trail of footprints.

For now, he merely asks, "Was it worth it?"

Eve turns to him, face alight, tears glimmering with the rainbow of new dawn. Nick's face, too, glows with awe.

"Yes," she whispers, for she'd do it a million times over.

A dog barks in the distance. Nick slides closer, wraps a warm arm around Eve's shoulders, and presses a kiss to her temple. Bathed in the splendor of dawn, he whispers, "Good morning."

MOVES LIKE JAGGER
Randi Perrin

Ian was the last one left in the office. With a pencil in each hand, he tapped out the drumbeat on the CD he was reviewing. The band's first album was significantly better than the new one and he flipped the case over to read the producer credits. Whoever it was needed to be hung out to dry for what he had done to the band's sound.

As it turned out, the lead singer was the producer for all but one of the tracks, and that lone song was the only one Ian remotely liked out of the bunch. He rolled his eyes and cracked his knuckles as he began to type.

Two years ago, the Flaming Pistons' debut album, Crankshaft, *set the music world on fire.*

Their latest venture, Shifting Gears, *is definitely a brand-new gear. In fact, they may not be driving the same car anymore. Their unique sound and gritty vocals as the star of each song, have been replaced by over-produced tracks (I hesitate to use the word "song" to describe them) that are too heavy on the drum machine and auto-tune.*

Musicians often hear, "don't quit your day job" when trying to make it in the music business but in this instance, Flaming Pistons' front man Jeremy "Monkey Wrench" McGraw needs to go back to his day job and just sing. I'm starting to understand why everyone calls him Monkey Wrench, because his creative vision definitely caused the band to throw a rod in a car that was barreling down the interstate at eighty miles-per-hour. On behalf of myself and everyone else in the universe, I beg you to leave the producing to the producers, Jeremy.

He gave the review one final look and sent the document to his editor who wouldn't look at it until after the holiday weekend.

The weekend was shaping up to be boring. Everyone was upstate to celebrate Christmas with their families, or busy with whatever other traditions they had. Ian didn't bother celebrating anymore— not since his parents ruined his holiday by telling him what a disappointment he was for following his passion and writing about others chasing their dreams of music. "It's a dead end, we just want to save you the disappointment later on," they'd said. He vowed to show them otherwise.

It had taken years of hard work and paying his dues at several smaller magazines, but by God, he'd done it. He was living the dream as a critic for *Rolling Stone.*

The phone on his desk rang. It never rang unless something horrible happened—a band's plane went down or his editor wanted to yell and scream over his latest article. He jerked the receiver off the cradle.

"Hello, this is a collect call from the North Pole. Do you accept the charges?"

Fully convinced it was a friend of his playing a holiday prank on him, he shrugged. "Sure."

A woman with a heavy British accent came on the phone. "Hello, Jagger Ian Brentwood?"

He rolled his eyes. No one called him by his first name—he wouldn't allow it. Growing up he was mocked far too much over the name his mother just *had* to bequeath to him because she had been "lucky" enough to meet the Rolling Stones while she was pregnant.

"It's Ian, but yes."

"If it's all the same, I'd like to call you Jagger."

"You and my mother," he muttered.

"Silly me, where are my manners? My name is Rhiannon. You may know me better as Mrs. Claus."

This is definitely one of my friends fucking with me.

"Abby, is that you? This isn't funny." Abby was the only one he knew capable of pulling off such a convincing accent. She was going to be in an off-Broadway production of *Mary Poppins* and had been practicing it a lot.

He picked up a pencil and banged it against the desk. *Tap. Tap. Tap.*

"No, my dear. This is not your friend Abby. I called you because I think we might be able to mutually benefit each other. I need your help with an unconventional request."

"No, no. I'm not into that." He paused and searched his mind for the right answer. "Besides, I've got a girl."

Across the crackling phone line, he could make out her laugh, and all of the tension he held in his shoulders dissipated as if her laughter had cast a spell over him.

"Jagger, I know you don't have a girlfriend. There's no need to lie to me."

"Who the hell are you?"

"All in good time, my dear. I'd like to invite you to my place tonight."

"You can't always get what you want."

"You might find that you get just what you need. There's a Town Car waiting for you downstairs," she said, then the line clicked and she was gone.

#

When Ian stepped out the door in his parka, his messenger bag slung across his chest, he was greeted by a gust of air so cold it made his eyes water. True to the stranger's word, a black Town Car with fully tinted windows was idling at the curb. He hesitated as he walked toward the vehicle—there was no way of knowing if he was getting into the car with a knife-wielding psycho or an insanely hot woman. Although his preference was on the latter, he was willing to bet money on the former.

A grateful breath blew past his lips when he climbed into the empty backseat and slipped his messenger bag over his head.

Not two minutes passed after the driver pulled away from the curb before he brought the car to a stop and motioned for Ian to get out.

"But we can't even have made it two blocks yet."

The driver shook his head with an amused *tsk, tsk.*

Frustrated, Ian shoved the door open and stepped into snow up to his knees. The moon was brighter and larger than he'd ever seen before, casting its light on the scene before him and a sign peeked out of the snow that read *North Pole.*

A horse carrying a tiny hobbit-looking creature on its back charged toward him. The animal kicked up snow that went up Ian's nose and into his eyes as it drew closer. The hobbit was wearing a tank-top and a pair of board shorts with loud neon colors and silhouettes of palm leaves all over them. Just looking at the hobbit made him shiver, even buried deep within his red parka.

"Aren't you cold?" Ian asked as he wrapped his arms around himself.

"Cold is but a state of mind," the hobbit said before he hopped down off the horse. Unlike Ian and the horse, his feet never broke through the surface of the snow and he walked toward Ian on top of it. "I'm Gorbadac, and I'll be your guide until we meet with Rhiannon."

"My guide? Are we going to run into Gollum while we're at it?"

Gorbadac shot him a look worthy of ice daggers flying across the moonlight. That was apparently the wrong damn thing to say.

"Look Mr. Know-It-All, just do what I say."

Ian nodded, worried if he talked back to him he might actually end up on a mission to destroy a ring in Mordor.

With a wicked smirk, the hobbit put his small, grizzled hands on his stocky hips. "Okay, walk in front of the horse and tell me what you see."

The little hobbit was insane. There was no need to walk in front of the horse—or hell, move at all—to know he was surrounded by snow as far as the eye could see. But when Ian turned around, the black Town Car that had deposited him in the snowy wasteland moments before was gone, as were any traces of it. No tire tracks, nothing. The only indication it had been there was Ian himself.

Ian threw his hands in the air. "I see snow. Lots and lots of snow."

The hobbit laughed. "Your perception is all wrong."

He held out his hand, fingers curled in a slight claw. With reluctance, Ian placed his hand in the hobbit's and was transported to a sandy beach. The horse frolicked in the surf, and sweat raced down Ian's spine.

"You won't be needing that anymore." With a snap of Gorbadac's haggard fingers, Ian's parka and messenger bag were gone, and his jeans were replaced by a pair of board shorts that were just as obnoxious as the hobbit's.

"Where is this place?" Ian turned a circle to take in his surroundings.

"This is the North Pole. The sign when you arrived told you that."

"But the snow, the ice…"

"The North Pole is a state of mind," Gorbadac replied, with a touch of *God-he's-stupid* dripping off his words. Ian wanted to kick the little dude to Mordor.

Ian put his hand up to stop him. "No, this is where Ozzy and I get off the Crazy Train. You already said cold is a state of mind. Are *you* a state of mind too?"

"This place, and everything about it, is whatever Rhiannon desires. This year it happens to resemble the Caribbean. Last year was Fiji. The year before that was turn-of-the-century Paris. Those who are not enlightened to our ways see ice and snow. It's a protection spell, to keep us safe."

"Spell?" Ian swallowed hard. The little jerk had denied his request to get off the train.

"Yes, dear, a spell."

His ears perked up at the same gorgeous accent that had beckoned him to this place. When Ian turned, a woman with wavy brown hair spilling over her shoulders was walking in his direction. She was dressed in a red velvet bikini with white cotton on the edges, like a vision from a naughty Santa's wet dream. A white satin robe dragged through the sand behind her.

"You're smart. I thought by now you'd have figured that much out."

"Not smart enough," he muttered while glancing over her curves. There were hot women to be found in every club and on every street corner of New York but the woman before him put all of them to shame. Never had Ian been tempted to use the word "perfect" to describe a woman, but that was the only word that came to mind. *Perfect tits. Perfect hair.* He snuck a look as a gust of wind caused the robe to billow around her. *Yup. Perfect ass.*

She couldn't have been a day over forty, and the only reason he was going with such a high number was because of the laugh lines that carved out tiny canyons around her glittering green eyes. Everything else about her screamed twenty-something and at the top of her game.

"You must be Rhiannon, goddess of the horse," he said, taking the hand she offered.

"Rhiannon, yes. Goddess, not so much. Just a normal, everyday witch. But I'm impressed with your research skills, Jagger."

He let go of her hand. "You're not going to call me Ian are you?"

She shook her head.

He gestured around. "Witchcraft isn't real, so the only logical solution here is that I'm dreaming."

She laughed. A hearty belly laugh that had her grasping at her midsection as the noise spilled from her shiny pink lips. It was a laugh he'd seen every winter from the Santa in Bloomingdale's. Or the one in Macy's. Or any of the stores he tried to avoid during the holiday season.

"I assure you that witchcraft is very much real and you're in the middle of it. You should be a bit more grateful that out of the seven billion people on the planet, I chose you for this task."

"Ch-chose me?"

Holy shit. I'm a sacrifice. Wait, if I was a sacrifice, wouldn't she have already killed me on an altar of my dignity or something like that? I must have slipped on the ice outside my building and hit my head and have one hell of a concussion. It's the only damn explanation. After all, how else can I explain a fuckin' hobbit in a neon bathing suit and a gorgeous Brit trying to convince me I'm in the North Pole?

Rhiannon watched as he worked through the logic, an amused look on her face. *Can she read my mind too?*

Ian shook his head and cleared his throat. "You're clearly delusional, and I've got to be on some wicked LSD trip or in a coma, but let's ride this out. If you are a witch—which you can't be, but let's pretend—what did you call me here for?"

"I have a problem, and I'm expecting you to be the solution. Time is of the utmost importance here." Her voice was practically sing-song, like Ian being the answer to all her problems was an everyday occurrence. "You said on the phone that you were Mrs. Claus. Just get your husband to fix it. Where is the old man, anyway? I want to give him a piece of my mind."

"You're right, I am Mrs. Claus. But Jagger, I'm not married and I never have been. Santa's not real."

"I know Santa's not real," he yelled. "I've known that since I was five when I caught my parents filling my stocking." He dragged his toes through the sand, kicking granules in the air with each swipe of his foot.

Leaning her lips close to his ear, she whispered, "The truth is, I need you. Without your help, Christmas as we know it won't happen. This year or ever again."

Ian shook his head, as if he was trying to shake her words from his memory bank. "I don't know which part of that sentence is the least believable—that I have any impact on Christmas whatsoever or that you need me." He stopped kicking up sand and planted his feet. "Why me?"

"Why not you? I've been watching you for a long time. I read *Rolling Stone*."

He broke out into a guffaw. "You read *Rolling Stone?* Is it delivered up here to your happy magic land?"

She laughed. "Of course not. But I have my ways—I see you when you're sleeping, I know when you're awake."

He rolled his eyes at the trite Christmas song lyrics. "Who is your favorite band, then? You strike me as an Indigo Girls kind of woman."

She leaned down to pick up a cracked seashell. As her fingers ran across it, the cracks disappeared and the shell became whole again. "They're good, but not my favorite. I'm partial to the Flaming Pistons. Their new album is fantastic. Magical, if you will."

"No. It's not."

"I do so love your opinions. So unique. Let me ask you something…did you listen to the lyrics to any of the songs on their latest album?"

No. Who could hear them over the drum machine and bass?

"Yeah, I just finished reviewing it."

"I know. Your takedown of them is epic, but if you listen to the lyrics, you might find something a bit deeper."

His eyes narrowed. *Does she intercept emails too?*

"How do you know about that review?"

"We've been over this before. Magic, m'dear." She gave an extra dramatic wave of her hand.

"If you're magic, why do you need me? You could just magic

whatever it is you need and leave me alone in my messy apartment with week-old pizza and even older Chinese take-out leftovers."

"I'll get to that in good time." She took his hand and tugged him along behind her toward a worn-out cottage hidden behind some coconut trees. "First, I think you need to better understand how Santa came to be. Only then can you understand my request."

"Oh, goody. Backstory," he deadpanned.

She stopped walking and narrowed her emerald eyes. "You may not care if Christmas comes or not—but there are millions of children who would. So, time to stop being an arrogant jerk and start thinking about someone else for a change."

Her tone had shifted to that of *don't-fuck-with-me*, and something told him she was not a person he wanted to cross. When she started walking again, he fell in line behind her. It wasn't like he had anywhere else to be.

"Jagger. How do you think Santa gets to every house in the world in one night?"

The weight of her stare bore down on him like an elephant crushing his chest. The cottage was much larger on the inside than the sad state of the exterior made it seem. The walls were covered in a honey-colored oak, and a giant fireplace filled the wall. It seemed so out-of-place in a beach cottage.

He dropped down onto the plush red couch on which she sat and dust swirled up around him. He made sure to leave the middle cushion between them—as if that tiny barrier of space could save him from her delusions of magical grandeur.

"He doesn't, because he's not real." Pride laced the answer to her trick question and he held his shoulders a little straighter.

"Incorrect," she snipped, snapping him from his reverie of intelligence.

"State of mind?" he asked, echoing Gorbadac's words from earlier. He was starting to worry about his own state of mind.

She shook her head. "Magic."

"But you just told me he wasn't real..." She stood and with a flick of her wrist, conjured a red velvet jacket that matched her bikini, with white puffs around the edges of the sleeves and hemline. The buttons were gold and polished to a high shine. She held it in one hand while her other moved around in the air. Inexplicably, though he hadn't moved, Ian found himself standing next to her. He slipped his arms into the sleeves; sparkles and dust swirled around him as the coat adjusted to his size, and his board shorts were replaced by a pair of matching and perfectly tailored trousers.

That was pretty damn cool.

She flicked her wrist again and her bikini was gone, replaced by a red velvet dress that was a perfect complement to the outfit he wore.

"What do you know of magic, Jagger?"

"I know it's not real... or at least I thought that was the case until about—" He looked at his watch. "Forty-five minutes ago."

"And how old do you think I am?"

He looked at his feet, which he'd just noticed were clad in shiny black boots, rather than try to look into her beautiful eyes. He knew, *just knew*, he was going to screw it up. The age question was a classic trap for a woman, like asking if her ass was too big. The best answer in either case was silence.

She tilted her head and gestured with her hands that she wanted an answer.

"Thirty? Maybe? Thirty-five, tops." He knew better than to say forty, like he'd thought earlier.

A low rumble of laughter erupted from her lips. "I am four hundred thirty-four years old."

"No way."

She smiled and her eyes crinkled. "Way. There's only one explanation. That is..."

"...that you're a liar," he said, finishing her sentence.

Snap!

He looked up at her face, which seemed miles away and was more distorted than gorgeous. Her smile had been replaced by a scowl.

It took a couple seconds for him to realize he was underwater, but something else was wrong. Even more wrong than being trapped underwater in a tropical North Pole with a self-proclaimed witch. His body was limp, as if his bones ceased to hold him together. An arm covered in suckers floated in front of his eye—*wait, just one?*—followed by another arm, and another.

She just turned me into a fucking octopus.

"Would you like to try again?" she asked, as she reached down and tapped her nail on the glass that separated their worlds, the sound reverberating through his cephalopod body.

Ian tried to speak, and couldn't, but his arms moved about, wildly searching for escape as if they each had minds of their own.

She snapped once again and he returned to his normal form, the red, velvet suit heavy with water that dripped onto the floor, forming a puddle around his feet.

"Now, would you like to give me a different answer this time?" she demanded.

"Why the fuck did you change me into an octopus, witchy woman?" he asked, choking on saltwater that burned the back of his throat.

Her lips twitched into a smile. "People who are resistant to accepting something new are weak and spineless. I was just giving you a body to go along with that."

"Ouch."

"Truth hurts, doesn't it?" Pursing her lips together, she blew a gentle breath over his shoulder and his clothes were dry.

"Wicked."

She waved her finger in the air. *Tsk. Tsk.* "No, not wicked. I'm a good witch. But a witch, nonetheless. And now we're all on the same page." She paced around the room, her high heels *click-clacking* on the hardwood floors. "It was a different time four hundred years ago.

We were in hiding. Witches and those who harbored them were killed by people who didn't understand them or didn't want to understand them. They just knew they were different and set out to rid the country of anyone who might have had an ounce of magic blood running through their veins."

"Sounds like not much has changed," he muttered.

With a wry smile, she walked over to him and sat down, her hands resting on his knee. "The enemy changes, but the fight is always there. Most humans are not capable of love in its purest sense— except at Christmas. That is when all the goodwill toward men peeks through. You know how they say there's magic at Christmas? It's not a lie."

That time he laughed. "Do you do find it just the slightest bit ironic that your pagan beliefs hinge on something so religious?"

"My dear boy, that's exactly why. Let me show you. What time and place would you like to visit, Jagger?"

He placed his finger to his chin and thought. There were so many options: the Berlin Wall coming down, Pearl Harbor, the building of the pyramids, Marie Antoinette's beheading.

"Take me to your most memorable childhood Christmas."

She let out a defeated sigh. "You don't want to see that. Surely there's something better you have in mind. Maybe the top of Mount Everest? Front row at a Bowie concert? To watch Michelangelo struggle on his back like a turtle at the Sistine Chapel?"

"Well...if you can't do it..."

"I can do it. I could even take you back to the Christmas where you threatened to run away because you didn't get a baseball mitt. What you don't know is that I had one for you. But you got in a fight with your brother two days before Christmas, and knocked out his tooth, so I kept it. It worked out for the best anyway."

The breath left his body, like a sucker punch to the gut. He'd never told anyone about wanting a baseball mitt so he could play with his big brother. He didn't get one, so he gave up that dream and turned to books and music. When he looked up at Rhiannon, she held out a child's baseball mitt adorned with a shiny red bow. On the tag, it read *To Jagger, From Santa. Knock it out of the park.*

Before he could speak again, she took his hand. With a flick of the wrist, they left the dreary expanse of snow behind, and instead stood in the shadows as they watched four little girls dressed in rags scurry around a fireplace in a tiny stone-walled cottage half the size of the one they'd been standing in a moment before. All the girls had the same full cheekbones, but only one, the oldest, had green eyes. He turned to look at his companion, but all the warmth in her face had been replaced by a stoic stare. She watched the younger version of herself with eyes that glistened in the flickers of light from the fireplace.

A blonde woman with the same striking eyes as Rhiannon, her hair pulled into a loose braid that fell down her back, tended to dinner over the fire, tears streaming down her face.

Her father pulled the younger girls close. "I love each and every one of you," he said. With a heavy sigh, he leaned back on the chair. The woman wrapped her arms around his neck and placed a gentle kiss in his hair. "I do not have Christmas gifts for the lot of you this year. Moving so many times to keep Rhiannon and your mother safe from the wolves has depleted everything I have." He dropped his head into his hands, his shoulders shaking.

All four of the little girls began to sob. Rhiannon's eyes spilled first. "Daddy, I don't want to be the reason everyone else suffers."

The blonde smiled at her, and patted her on the head. "Your heart has always been big, my sweet Rhiannon. I just fear one day it will destroy you." She walked away to tend to dinner once again.

The youngest of the girls grabbed Rhiannon's hand and looked up, a trail of tears cutting through the dirt on her cheek. "I would rather go without Christmas presents than a sister."

Shaking his head, Ian looked up into the adult Rhiannon's knowing eyes. Where at first he hadn't seen more than a few wrinkles around them, he realized they were, in fact, eyes that had seen it all. Pain, love, sacrifice, and understanding.

"Have you seen enough?" she whispered.

He nodded, and she flicked her wrist, returning them to the sunny beach, and their beach attire.

Waves lapped at his feet, soaking through his blue Chuck Taylors. "Why don't you take credit for what you do?"

"It was a different time then, and to do anything, I needed to be wed. I had no desire to be tethered to a man—be it through love, obligation, or anything else—so I made one up. I could do things the way I wanted, and give all the credit to someone else."

"The elves, the magic reindeer? What about them?"

She clapped her hands and silhouettes of eight reindeer danced around in the sky, before they dissipated into nothing. "Those? Merely folklore. I get bored, I add a new story to the myth."

"Do you just magic all the toys?"

"You trivialize it but it is all done with magic, yes. Gorbadac is a warlock." She held up a finger. "Not a hobbit."

"Sorry," he mumbled. *Not sorry.*

"The persecution went on for years. Thousands of witches were slain for the blood that courses through them. The gift that makes us stand apart from humans became the curse we tried to hide. I provide witches and warlocks with a safe haven. Not all of them, mind you, but a good many of them. If they promise to help fulfill my mission, I give them an environment to utilize and perfect their gifts as opposed to suppressing them. In this place we all work together to make the world a better place, even if it is but for one night out of a year. But..." she trailed off and dropped her eyes to her feet.

"But what?"

"There's an illness that has affected most of the witches and warlocks. It slowly drains the magic from their body until there is nothing left to distinguish them from mere humans. Once their magic is gone, they no longer see my vision for this world, they only see snow and darkness and have no way of escape. Even Gorbadac has fallen victim. His magic is weak. It's been diminishing for weeks now, and there isn't much time left to save him. I fear that I will be next."

"Are you sure we're talking about the same hob—warlock? Because he changed my clothes and switched between snow and this beach just fine."

She let out a deep exhale. "Jagger, that is peasant magic. Even the youngest of witches with the tiniest inklings of powers can perform those parlor tricks." She turned and walked back in the direction of the cottage. He jogged up behind her, which was difficult to do in water-logged sneakers.

"Where do I fit in? I can't do magic. I'm not a doctor. I listen to music for a living."

"I need you to fetch me Monkey Wrench's wife. It's that easy. Go get her and bring her to me. The Flaming Pistons are doing a fan-club pre-release listening party at the club down the street from your apartment. She should be there."

He raised an eyebrow. "So, now I'm adding kidnapping to my resume?"

She laughed, a deep hearty laugh that made her shoulders bounce as she tried to muffle the sounds. "Not at all. But I warn you, she won't come willingly. Whatever you do, don't use my name."

"No pressure, huh?"

"I wouldn't ask for your help unless I knew you could do it." She flicked her wrist and a fan-club badge on a lanyard covered in flames appeared around his neck. "That should get you into the party. Everything else is up to you."

"How am I going to get home? The car is long gone."

"The same way we visit millions of children in one night." She put her hand on the mantle of the gigantic fireplace and the useless logs transformed into the lonely bedroom of his apartment. The bed hadn't been made and dirty laundry exploded from the hamper.

His eyes grew wide and his lips turned up into a smile. It was so simple, so voyeuristic, and so freakin' cool. It definitely got around the pesky problem of millions of kids without chimneys for Santa to shimmy down.

"How will I get back?"

She placed a snow globe in his hands. When he peered closer, beneath the swirling glitter and water, he recognized himself and Rhiannon standing in the middle of a room together.

"Both you and she must place your right hands on the glass and sing a Christmas song. Tap the glass three times with your middle finger, and think about falling into the scene beneath your hands. If you do it right, you'll transport from New York to here."

"And if I do it wrong?"

She shook her head. "Do you believe in me?"

If he were honest, the jury was still out on that. "I believe in magic."

Her lips curled into a wicked smile. "That's good. Because every little thing I do is magic. It's up to you to keep it that way." She rested her perfectly manicured hand with bright red nails on his shoulder. "Now, go get me what I want for Christmas."

Her crimson red lips landed on his cheek, and then she pushed him into the fireplace.

Stumbling back against his bed, Jagger looked around at the mess that was his room, his life, and let out a sigh of disappointment. He was back in reality, with a mission and no idea how to pull it off. And he was still in the loud board shorts and wet shoes. It seemed that more than just his old world view had been left in the North Pole—his pants and red parka had too. *It's what Bloomingdale's exists for, right?*

Entering his bedroom on the hunt for clothes to change into, he was shocked to find his jeans and parka neatly folded on his bed. Next to them was his leather messenger bag. He changed, and then slipped on his parka, and patted the pockets. "Oh shit, where the hell did that snow globe go?" He didn't remember letting go of it before his tumble through Rhiannon's fireplace, but it wouldn't be the strangest thing to happen to him that night.

Pulling his laptop out of the bag, he was relieved to see the snow globe at the bottom. He slid the leather strap over his head and walked out his apartment, slamming the door behind him.

He clambered down the sixteen flights of stairs, taking them two at a time, and burst out onto the cold street through a side door instead of going through the lobby. It was better that his doorman, Dwight, didn't stop him with stories about his kids. Not that night.

He sucked a breath of freezing air, burning his lungs, before he took off at a jog down the street toward the club. *I'm getting too old for this shit.* Ian reached the venue and groaned. There was a line and it wasn't moving. With a sigh, he looked around for another way in.

A sign with an arrow that pointed to the VIP entrance was almost hidden behind a bouncer who resembled a body builder who ate another body builder. With a single tug, Ian broke the clasp on the lanyard around his neck, buried it deep into his messenger bag, and stepped out of line. His half-baked plan involved walking by the bouncer like he was just a passerby instead of some lame-o who couldn't make it to a show on time.

As he took cautious steps past the giant at the door, his heart thundering in his ears, the bouncer zeroed in on him.

"Jagger. Jagger Brentwood. Get over here, man." The bouncer wrapped his giant arm that was covered in some tribal tattoo from wrist to shoulder—the fact he was sleeveless in twenty degree weather didn't seem to phase him in the least—around Ian's neck and pulled him close. "I haven't seen you in years, man."

"I don't know how you know my name, but I don't know who you are."

The bouncer smiled and showed off his pearly white teeth that stood out in the darkness. "You always were so funny." He slipped a VIP lanyard over Ian's neck and gave him a shove. "You go on inside now. Just consider it a gift from Santa."

❄

Now that I'm inside, what the hell am I going to do?

The room was packed with people. If it wasn't over capacity, his name wasn't—*shudder*—Jagger.

With a push here and a shove there, he made his way to the front of the pseudo-mosh pit that had formed, and looked up onto the stage. All four members of the band were dressed in jeans and ugly Christmas sweaters. Someone took playing two days before Christmas a little too seriously.

Standing a mere ten feet from Monkey Wrench, he was mesmerized by the singer's fingers as they flew across the neck of the guitar, eliciting a sound that, at least to his ears, had always been magic.

A flick of your wrist, a wave of your hand
Changes direction, the hourglass sand
Those magic things you do, hidden from view
I thought you were magic when my eyes first found yours
Little did I know there was so much more
Locked away, hidden from view
Bring it out baby, show me your magic side
There's no one watching, no need to hide

The song's lyrics hit Ian like a freight train—Monkey Wrench's wife was a witch. No wonder Rhiannon wanted her. But for what?

Ian focused intently on the people off-stage. That's when he noticed a woman, her hair falling over her shoulders in golden waves, who was almost as pretty as Rhiannon, even though she was wearing the same ugly sweater as Monkey Wrench.

Ian fought his way through the crowd toward backstage. The show would be wrapping up soon and just as the clock was ticking off the minutes until Christmas Eve, it was also ticking off each second of opportunity he had to save Rhiannon.

With each wail from the guitar and each scream that erupted from the crowd, Ian grew more frustrated. There wasn't a way out of the sea of people, and even if he found one, he still had to get past the wall of bouncers protecting the stage.

Just then, someone fell into him, and their drink sloshed out of the glass and all over Ian's back. Jerking upright and trying to ignore the line of what smelled like vodka that slithered down his back, Ian turned to give the clumsy fool a piece of his mind.

And came face-to-face with his editor, Killian.

"Hey man, I didn't expect to see you tonight," his editor said. His words were much more coherent than Ian expected given the eau d'alcohol he wore. "I mean, you ripped the CD, why are you here?"

"Someone suggested I give it another chance."

A pretty girl with raven-colored hair wrapped her arms around Killain's waist but he shook her free. "Not right now, baby." He looked up at Ian with a smile. "It's not like you to give a band a second shot—especially at Christmas."

"Let's just say my Grinchlike heart grew three sizes today, okay? You don't mind tossing out that review and pretending like you never saw it?"

"What review?"

Ian smiled.

"Would you like to go meet the band?" Killian asked.

"How in the hell are you going to pull that off?"

Killian tugged the dark-haired girl close. "It pays to date their producer's daughter."

Backstage, Killian's girlfriend introduced them all around and the final person Ian was introduced to was Sybil, Monkey Wrench's wife.

"Pleased to meet you," she said as she took his hand. She spoke slowly, as if she was trying hard to form the words. If he didn't know any better, he'd swear she was trying to suppress an accent.

"The pleasure is all mine," he said as he released her hand. "Tell me, how long have you and Monkey Wrench been together?"

She gave him a wide smile and he was nearly blinded by her teeth. "His name is Jeremy, and we've been together a long time."

Jeremy came up behind her and nuzzled his face against her neck. "When your years are as magical as ours, you tend to lose track of time."

Ian smiled. *Monkey Wrench knows.*

"You're the *Rolling Stone* reviewer who loved our first album, right?" Jeremy asked.

Ian nodded. "Yes. Still trying to develop an opinion about this one. This party was my second listen."

"How about we go do a few shots in my dressing room? Maybe we can loosen you up and sway your opinion."

It was a bribe, but Ian was not one to turn down free liquor—or a chance to be in the same room as the target of his mission to save Christmas.

Jeremy slipped his hand into his wife's and Ian followed behind like a puppy on a string as they moved away from the crowd.

In his dressing room, Jeremy pulled out a brand-new bottle of Dom Perignon and poured a glass that he handed to Sybil. He held up the bottle toward Ian.

"No, that's pussy stuff," Ian said with a laugh.

"I like this guy," Jeremy said as he pulled out a bottle of Kentucky bourbon. It wasn't Ian's favorite, but he'd choke it down if it bought him a few more minutes. The sacrifices he was willing to make for a beautiful stranger all in the name of Christmas.

Jeremy handed Ian a double shot and they tossed them back. Ian hadn't even set his shot glass down before it was being refilled.

Ian rummaged through his bag. "Sybil, do you like to sing?"

She shrugged. "I am not any good. That is why Jeremy is the famous one, not me."

Palming the snow globe in his right hand, he glanced at the clock, which read ten minutes after midnight. "It's Christmas Eve now. I thought we might sing some Christmas music."

"How about 'Jingle Bells,'" Jeremy suggested. "I love that one." He picked up a guitar and strummed a few chords.

Ian smiled. "Perfect." He stepped toward Sybil as his mouth started to form the words that were engrained in his head since childhood despite his desires to the contrary.

Ian handed the globe to Sybil, but kept his right hand on it. He tapped his finger three times expecting something to happen.

Nothing happened except Sybil singing about what fun it was to ride whores for a roll in the hay. The snow globe crashed to the floor sending shards of glass, water, and glitter everywhere.

"What were you doing?" Sybil demanded, her hands on her hips.

"Singing, same as you were," he said, feigning innocence.

Mist rose from the shattered snow globe and wrapped around their ankles.

"He has magic," Sybil screeched. "I feel it dragging me down. You're not really a reviewer, are you?"

Ian nodded. "I am. It's all I've ever wanted to be." The call to offer him the job came in right around Christmas two years before.

Sybil's eyes narrowed and her brow furrowed. She wasn't very pretty when she was pissed off. "Then why do you have magical artifacts?"

He pointed to the ground and kicked some of the broken glass at his feet. "That old thing? A stranger gave it to me."

"You lie."

Jeremy lifted his hands and waved his right in the air, making large circles until a gray cloud formed in the air above them. He dropped his hands and lightning cracked down, striking each of them.

Ian, Jeremy, and Sybil landed in a heap in the sand. Gorbadac stood off to the side, his shoulders bouncing with what Ian assumed was laughter, though it sounded more like a screeching baboon.

"A little help here," Ian called to the miniature warlock.

Gorbadac held up his hands and snapped, but all that happened was that his ugly board shorts changed into a bright yellow speedo. The hobbit lookalike clasped his hands over his banana hammock, and his cheeks burned bright red.

"Really?" Ian yelled. "That was helpful."

Gorbadac shook his head and snapped again. Nothing happened. He snapped again, and still nothing. His magic was gone, and at the most inopportune time, leaving everyone with quite the view. The disappointment and guilt that ripped through Ian was foreign and frightening. *I can't believe I didn't make it on time.*

Rhiannon ran out of the cottage and met them all on the shore.

"This isn't where you were supposed to wind up," Rhiannon said, her voice an octave above normal.

"I did everything right, even the singing Christmas carols," Ian grunted as he stood.

Rhiannon laughed. "That wasn't going to do anything but make both of you look like fools. It was certainly entertaining. The snow globe was only to give Jeremy the signal and location to activate a portal."

Jeremy stood up and dusted the sand off himself. "I hope this is worth the ass-chewing I'm going to get later."

"I have taught you well," she said as she wrapped her arms around Jeremy in a friendly embrace.

Sybil stood up and glared at Rhiannon. The icy stare Rhiannon shot back told Ian this meeting was not a happy reunion. No wonder she said not to mention her name.

"Hello, Mother," Rhiannon said.

Ian's mouth fell open.

"Why have you beckoned me here?" Whatever accent Sybil had been trying to hide earlier was on prominent display, and was thicker than Rhiannon's.

"I'm at your mercy," Rhiannon said as she fell to her knees. "There is an illness that has spread to all of my witches and warlocks, and it has begun to take its toll on me. I can do many things, but I am no healer."

Sybil gave a dismissive wave. "There are others."

"None as powerful as you. I'm humbly asking you to save those in this safe place I've worked so hard to create. Do it for Christmas. Do it for your kind. Do it for your daughter."

Sybil laughed. "Ha. Safe place? They no longer persecute witches. You should try stepping out of your 'safety' bubble, you and your slaves."

Gorbadac stepped forward. "It is nothing of the sort. We are all here willingly." He snapped his fingers, but nothing happened. He tried again to the same results. "We can leave at any moment, just as you did."

Guilt pricked at Ian. It had been years since he'd travelled to Pennsylvania to visit his parents. Would they harbor the same resentment Sybil had?

Sybil rolled her eyes. "Are you guilt-tripping me?"

"Is it working?" Rhiannon asked.

"I'll fix your pathetic little coven, but I will not stay. I do not like this world, being at the mercy of your state of mind." Jeremy took a reticent step closer to his wife and whispered in her ear. Sybil grimaced and continued. "However, if it will please you, I will release the protections that close my world to your fireplace of voyeurism. You will be free to visit in *our* world once a year at Christmas, seeing as how we're family and it's your holiday and all."

Rhiannon smiled. "I'd like that very much, Mother."

Sybil took a deep breath, closed her eyes, and stretched her arms out on either side of her body. Power escaped her fingertips in tiny sparks as she began to shake. She brought her hands together and held them over each other until a ball of light formed between her palms, and then she pushed the light toward the heavens. As her lips formed the words of her incantation, a dome of light surrounded them all.

Ye goddess, hear my plea
Heal these witches that surround me
This plague shall never return here again
Or any land under the eye of Rhiannon
Return their power, lift this curse
So it shall be, when I finish this verse

She collapsed into Jeremy's waiting arms as she completed the incantation. The light that surrounded them pulsed from white to red, then blue, and finally green.

"It is done," Sybil whispered, clearly drained of power as Jeremy held her steady.

"Thank you," Rhiannon whispered.

"Merry Christmas," Sybil replied. "Now, I believe they have work to do." She tilted her head in the direction of the crowd of witches, which had already started to disperse. "Take me home, Jeremy."

With Sybil in his arms, Jeremy stepped through the giant fireplace to return to their fancy penthouse on the upper East side.

Next up, it was time for Ian to return to reality, and for a place he refused to acknowledge the day before, he found himself longing not to leave.

Rhiannon wrapped her arms around him in a hug. "Thank you. You have not only saved Christmas, my witches and warlocks, but also a relationship I feared would never be repaired. I told you that you were the one for the job. You deserve what you've always wanted for Christmas."

He tilted his head to the side. "And what is that?"

Rhiannon smiled. "Your heart knows," she whispered before she pushed him through the fireplace.

He stared at the blank white wall of his bedroom and sighed. He knew he'd never see Rhiannon again—yet his life would never be the same. All thanks to a phone call.

A phone call!

In the living room he turned on his laptop to rewrite his review.

He played the CD again, paying special attention to the lyrics, inflection, and even over-production.

Two years ago, the Flaming Pistons came out of the gate strong with their debut album, Crankshaft, *setting the music world on fire.*

Their latest venture, Shifting Gears, *is definitely a brand-new gear. Their sound has been enhanced by an extra drum loop, stronger vocals, and nine tracks that are a detour from their first album with lyrics that allude to magic, hope, love, and sacrifice, all wrapped in metaphor. This is definitely an album that deserves a second (or third) listen before final judgment is placed.*

Flaming Pistons' front man Jeremy "Monkey Wrench" McGraw shared co-producing credits on nine of the tracks. Already a strong leader with his one-of-a-kind song lyrics and gritty delivery, he can add another layer of creative vision to his already unique repertoire.

Now that they are barreling down the interstate at eighty miles-per-hour, it will be interesting to see where they end up after this detour— will they circle back to their roots or will they take us on an even more wily adventure?

With a final read through, he attached the review to an email and sent it off to his editor, and then he picked up his phone.

With fumbling fingers, he dialed the number he'd written on girls' hands, napkins, or notebooks countless times during high school.

"Hello?" The voice was sleepy, and he noticed it was a after one in the morning. *Whoops.*

"Merry Christmas, Mom."

"Paul, is that you? Why are you calling me at this ungodly hour?"

He took a deep breath. "No, Mom, it's not Paul."

"Jagger?"

"Yeah, it's Jagger. I just wanted to wish you a Merry Christmas, and see if, maybe you'd be willing to come up for a visit next week. I'll see if I can pull some strings for *Hamilton* tickets, maybe go ice skating at Rockefeller, go to Times Square on New Year's Eve so you can see Ryan Seacrest."

"Oh honey, he's no Dick Clark. But we'd love to. Merry Christmas, Jag. I love you."

"I love you, too," he whispered just before the line clicked.

A rumble shook his belly and he realized he hadn't eaten in more than twenty-four hours. He was starving—ready to eat through the two-foot tall sandwich at the deli on the corner. Thank goodness it was always open.

He went to the elevator and pushed the button ten times, as if the fact it was lit up didn't mean a thing. When the doors opened up, he was alone with the bellhop, who eyed him cautiously.

"Come on Gary, I only had a panic attack the one time. Relax, I'll be okay."

"Whatever you say," Gary muttered before he pressed his gloved finger on the button for the ground floor.

Ian stepped out of the elevator humming "Santa Claus is Coming to Town," and then moved onto "Jingle Bells." He stopped at the cluster of mailboxes to collect the bills and Christmas cards he'd been ignoring for the past week.

He pulled out the pile of envelopes and a bright green one on top with no postage and a return address of N.P. caught his attention. He flipped it over and opened it up. There was no note, nothing but three tickets to see *Hamilton*. Good seats, too.

It's good to know a witch.

MISS 'LIL TOE HEAD
Michael Leonberger

I kiss Santa in an old Chevy parked under a sputtering orange street light, and beneath the coiling silver beard whiskers, Santa's actually a girl.

True story. Scout's honor.

Even with the beard and the make-up, I can tell because of her lips and eyes. I think she's got the most mesmerizing lips and eyes in the world, even if they look through you sometimes, even if they stare into nothing, even if those lips spend too much time curled into a frown. They give it away, tell the whole story of a sad and charming prize, my misfit I found at the bottom of a Cracker Jack box.

We trudge out into a night air that's too warm for December, that threatens a light rain whose droplets will never become snowflakes. The sky's a dim gray light bulb smothered in black paint, punched out all over with the chaos of Christmas lights below. Reds and greens, twinkling like merry gunshot wounds, bleeding cheer.

She did a good job with her make-up: she used spirit gum to keep the beard in place, and folded liquid latex into creases around her mouth and eyes. Used creams to give her cheeks and nose that ruddy, jolly, slightly demented drunk look, like old St. Nick. Everyone's favorite alcoholic uncle.

She's got a small body, all wire and Teflon, but the uniform she wears is padded in all the wrong places: bulbous Santa throughout, cascading down her flat chest and caricaturing her sculpted behind.

I follow her from her old Chevy to the address: dutiful Mrs. Claus following behind her man, and my make-up is quite a bit less impressive. Just lipstick and rouge and stuff around my eyes to pull them out, like a slap-happy drunk elf, and I smile like the housebound fool I am. Tonight I'll stay in the background. I complete the Santa package, and we'll make more money off of my presence, but sometimes I'm sort of a liability for Santa.

I mean, not in this neighborhood.

In this neighborhood, most people don't mind a brown Mrs. Claus, but they do in other parts of this shit heap I call my home. And despite the fact our acting chops are similar, no one has ever hired a brown Santa, with or without a white Mrs. Claus.

Were they to ever look past her make-up and discover they were hiring two Mrs. Clauses, our holiday income might dry up entirely.

But they haven't so far, and so here we are.

I'll giggle, and she'll "Ho, ho, ho" and I can still taste her kiss. It's the best part of the holiday. Christmas isn't the smell of fire places in the cold. Not for me. Not anymore, if it ever was. And it isn't a mouthful of that chemical craft store odor, either, or vanilla scented candles.

No, the smell and taste of Christmas is something altogether more intimate. Embarrassing and terrific. The pine sap of those Christmas trees people sing about is comically inadequate.

"Ho, ho, ho!" she bellows as the charming young couple open the front door. They look nice enough, even if I intrinsically dislike them and I figure they sold their soul to Satan to afford this ghoulish mansion. Even if I believe somewhere in my rotten guts that these are cheap, plastic smiles that live behind expensive, manicured lawns.

I see wounds here, in the good life.

All ferociously judgmental, because I tell myself I'll never know this life.

My couch has a bad spring. I love to feel it in my back when we fuck, and if you run your fingers along that spot on my skin I'll probably cum right away from muscle memory. It folds out into a bed, but the couch is more comfortable, so that's where we screw and sleep, until the feeling of another person breathing down your neck keeps you up all night, and you've got no choice but to sleep on the floor. I figure we're real people because of all this. I'm proud of it in some adolescent way and I resent this couple who've hired us for what they don't know. And I know I'm full of shit.

I am.

Anyway, I smile, because it's Christmas.

I bat my fake eyelashes, giggle at their happiness ("You two look terrific! They'll be so thrilled!"), wonder if they suspect we're dating, that this is less of an act than either one of them know. That I'm exhausted with myself.

We sneak into the living room, up to the tree, and Santa drops her bulging sack of presents to the floor. It's warm and dimly lit, so those low burning Christmas lights really make me feel nostalgic.

My dad loved Christmas. Very American, he said.

If only you could see me now.

Flames crackle drowsily in the fire place—it's much too warm for a fire, but it *is* Christmas after all—and two stockings hang above the fire place. They make me sad for reasons I can't explain.

No. I can, though.

I feel embarrassed by them. I think that's what it is. It would be embarrassing to ever have to wear socks that long, don't you think? It doesn't make sense, but it's my honest thought. The way the candy has collected at the bottom makes it seem like the feet are all mashed up in there, bound and ruined like the feet of ancient women in China.

There's nothing wrong with this holiday, you know, but there's something wrong with me.

I look at Santa. She's giving me a warm, jolly, Santa Claus gaze (she's the better actor, I'm telling you). I'm glad she's here. I'm always glad when she's here, because it grounds me. Sometimes I feel like I might just fly away, but she anchors me. Pulls me down with her confident, strong hands.

I wish those hands could pull me down all the time.

I wish she could pull me down tomorrow, on Christmas Day.

But she's heading back home tonight, and I'll be spending the holiday alone.

I'm starting to miss her already.

"Ho, ho, ho!"

It really is a thrill when the kids come galloping out of their bedrooms, after the gentle suggestion of their parents ("Santa's here! He's downstairs now! Hush now, he'll hear you!"). You hear them stomping down the halls, whooping and hollering in that unselfconscious way kids do. Thrilled to see us from the distance of the banister.

They're not embarrassed by the stockings, of course.

I hear Mom and Dad urging them to be quiet ("Don't let them hear you!") and I love that they think they're stealthy. Two little James Bonds. And I like that Mrs. Claus is brown to them, and will be for a long time ("Guys, we saw them though! With our own eyes!")

But then a small part of me wonders: is this a violence?

The lie.

The older one, he was probably about ready to let this whole thing go. But now he's seen us, in the flesh and he'll probably stay a child for just a little bit longer. So either it's magic, or we just ripped the stitches out of a wound that'll take a longer time to heal, probably scar funny and boil into the kind of resentment you get when your parents lie to you.

I wonder if he'll resent the two of us for lying, too.

We get paid for it, though. Cold cash, and then we pile back into our sex Chevy and Santa has the decency to finger me along the way (*"Ho, ho, ho"*). She swerves only a little as I shudder and buckle against my seatbelt, locking against my chest.

The Lord is come.

Christmas time is here.

It's midnight and Christmas and we're in that magic wasteland of wires and dusty cinder, all gutted floors and the corpse of what used to be a bowling alley. The Missile. Our spot.

The lanes are untouched, even if the old arcade is now a hole in the ground filled up with rebar, all snapped ribs from where time pulled itself out of the alley's womb. It left us the husk and we are grateful.

The barstools have been plucked from the bar like baby teeth, but two remain, and they're ours. We sit at that empty bar, and look into the cavernous floor behind it, where machinery has been removed, leaving behind big, empty squares in the ground like unoccupied graves.

I help her peel away the latex and spirit gum. Swab away the flaky tendrils left over with make-up remover wipes, and now she's smiling at me, fresh faced, beardless and somehow more alive for the raw pink blemishes in her skin illuminated by the shafts of moonlight that rain down like cold Christmas napalm through holes in the ceiling. Santa no more, the hot licks of short red hair on top of her head revealing the true color the silver coils tried to hide.

Christmas miracle, I think to myself as I stomp to the empty bathrooms at the perimeter of The Missile and throw those wipes in a dry toilet that's become a trash can. When I come back I see her stripped of her Santa costume. It's draped along the counter and she's sitting on top of it, legs set wide apart, feet planted on our bar stools. She's only wearing a sports bra and a smile, her legs wide open, holding that piece of mistletoe above her head and shimmying her shoulders back and forth with mischief. I could watch her shimmy for an eternity.

That mistletoe's a gift I got her—special mistletoe for a special kiss. It sort of started as a gag.

She started calling me "Toe Head" when I bleached my hair in November. It's blond and in curls like Marilyn Monroe, and I can dim my eyes the way Marilyn did, too. I promise. That sleepy, sexy come-on that puts the color in old black and white films. It's done good things for my sex life with Santa, who's coiling her fingers through my hair now, as I stoop my shoulders by the bar and kiss her where she wants it.

"Missile, Toe Head," she said on the phone one day, and I giggled and felt warmth in my stomach.

"What did you call me?"

"I didn't call you anything," she teased. "Can you meet me at The Missile?"

"Thought you called me Miss 'Lil Toe Head...'"

I couldn't hide what I wanted in my voice, and she snorted soda pop on the other end of the phone.

"I can call you that and I will call you that," she laughed, and she's been calling me that ever since.

So actual Mistletoe Head seemed the logical next step. A couple's Christmas gift, and here we are.

"When I was a kid," she says, struggling with the words, eyes rolled back and holding onto my head for support. "We got to open a present early, on Christmas Eve. But now it's Christmas. So Merry Christmas, Miss 'Lil Toe Head."

I don't speak. I'm busy teasing the bow of my present with my tongue.

❆

Afterwards, she roots around in the dark for our bowling balls, which stay undigested in the back of the mouths of the lanes. The machinery that returns the balls hasn't worked for a long time now.

I set up our empty beer bottle pins, then crack open two fresh ones. They open with a hiss and a frosty white exhalation, we clink beers and she's up first. The pins go down with the satisfying clonk of glass, all recycling cans and garbage shoots, and then I'm up. I slip off my shoes (no socks, no bowling shoes) and the ground is cold against my heels. I feel my bum toe, the baby one on my right foot, which murmurs sweet numb nothings to me as I walk. I can't feel it even though I can, and it's become my favorite part. Bowling barefoot. That phantom reminder, something like the physical tingle of regret.

There's something wrong with me, I guess.

"Miss 'Lil Toe Head!" she exclaims eagerly as my ball sails straight into the gutter. I pout, then pound down the lane, knocking the bottles down with my feet. "A surprising strike," she corrects, and I'm grinning from ear to ear.

Then we climb on top of the gutted bathroom stalls. Step on the sink, then the hand driers, peel back that bad tile in the ceiling, and *wam-o!*—it's up on the rooftop.

She's up first, disappearing into the ceiling, reaching her hand back through that hole, and I pass the six pack up to her. I climb up next and the air is surprisingly chill when I pull myself through.

"Miss 'Lil Toe Head, my 'Lil wack-a-mole," she says as I climb through, gently bopping me on the head.

Then we huddle up near the edge, unscrewing new beers, toasting to the night, with its cornucopia of colors, with its Christmas silence, all sleeping babies waiting for Santa, and no one knows she's actually up here with me.

No one knows.

I nuzzle her neck. Hold her tight, because I know she has to leave soon.

She fans her toes out on the edge of The Missile rooftop, and the moon really brings out her scars.

Like thin little silver toe rings, white slivers at the base of seven of her ten toes.

This is her brilliance.

I'll be working two shifts tomorrow (no family for Christmas and no money, either, makes Mrs. Claus an absent working elf mom), but Santa isn't working *at all.*

No, she gets a happy check every time she lets the medical students at Winston University remove one of her toes and reattach it. Putting them back on is practice for them, and she signs a waiver that essentially says if the feeling never returns, she won't return, either. With a lawyer. Suing. That sort of thing.

I signed up for the surgery once. A happy check that bought me our happy couch, but the feeling never came back for me.

I look at my baby toe, with its scarred looking toe ring, and it's like staring at a stranger. I wiggle it, but it's someone else waving back. My constant humming companion, a torn nerve that won't heal.

It's weirdly satisfying.

She swears hers are all fine. And I swear mine is fine, too. That kind of a secret keeps me more secure in my own head, even if it doesn't do much for our relationship.

Unless we're both lying.

She takes part in tests and experiments all the time to make money. Has had more violent and strange sicknesses coarse through her little body than I really care to know. It seemed exotic and forbidden when we first met.

When I didn't love her.

Now that I do, I wish she'd stop. All those waivers pile up tall and start looking like a tombstone. Honestly. And the missing is too hard.

I'm reminded of that when Stevie pulls up outside the Missile and honks. She pops out with her short blond hair, shaved at the sides, perfect on the top, and I think she looks better than me, waving up at us.

The missing is hard when Santa climbs into the front seat and disappears into the night together with another girl, back home, heading towards Christmas, and I'm a widowed Mrs. Claus watching them go. All that was willed to me is the rest of this six pack.

That bitterness combined with the light beer and the soft glaze of Christmas lights eventually takes my thoughts to my dad.

It's a familiar train of thought for me on Christmas.

My toe is my secret monument to him.

I used to sit up on a stool in his basement and watch him work.

It was his basement as much as it was Mom's kitchen. She didn't want to come down and he didn't want to go up. All North Pole, South Pole and I spent my time scurrying between the two, Father and Mother and all the icy silence between them, and I could never be enough to fill all of that. Especially because I was very small. Especially because I was probably the one who caused the blizzard in the first place.

But still I'd try, a mad Rudolph hauling something shrill and horrible back and forth, all the weight of the knowing that those empty staircases were mine. My birthright, what I deserved. Whatever they'd been together before I came along was just a phantom limb now and the missing was too hard for them too, I think.

Then there's me: the missing made flesh, Miss 'Lil Missing.

Mom would roll her eyes at that. So it's back down to the basement, then, back to the workshop, because Dad didn't roll his eyes at me.

He didn't.

Dad always lit up when I came down. Sat me on a bench and called me his little elf. The warm, electric smell of sawdust flittering through the air is something I can't handle.

The way the sawdust settled in the blood that day is something I'll never forget.

The way he was screaming, after the saw ate through his arm.

The fact that I now know he was lying.

His smiles of relief when it was all said and done, his brow spotted with sweat and those sleepy, dopy smiles, because it was gone. His arm.

It's gone, it's gone, it's gone...

Because he'd made it seem like an accident. Like he accidentally sawed his own arm off.

But I know the truth.

It was no accident. The way he explained it to me, later, before he left, was that it was as though his arm had always been off. Doctors call it *body identity integrity disorder.* That he felt he'd been born with an extra arm, an appendix that shouldn't have been there. That he'd dreamed his whole life of being rid of it, of being the person he was supposed to be.

And how do you explain that? To a child, to a little elf?

So he didn't explain it. He just made it an accident.

My little elf. You look good in red.

And I don't know that I had to see it lying there in the sawdust. The blood gushing from him. I don't know that I had to see it for his lie to have worked, and that's where my hatred for him comes from.

No, I don't think I had to see it, and I don't think I'll ever forgive him for that, even if I want to understand.

I waggle my toe and I think I understand, and I resent that all I get from my father any more is a post card on Christmas. No return address. He thinks I want him to stay away, because that guilt and self-loathing makes the whole thing easier for him.

But it doesn't make anything easier for me, and I don't want him to stay away. I want him here, so I can scream at him. Scream into his face and tell him the whole thing isn't okay, that I'm not okay, that the scars I've got inside are on the outside now, too.

That I've got one, myself. My stupid, little toe.

That I love him, too. That I don't want him to just be a phantom limb.

I want to say all of those things, but instead I let it rage in my head, where I guess it raged for him his whole life. I let it rage, and I drink the rest of the beers quietly, because that's what you do.

That's what you're supposed to do.

It's in my pocket and I pull it out: the postcard, all chicken scratch lettering, like the home made gifts he'd make when I was a kid. Mom got it right: she'd get me Malibu Barbie and plastic mansions for her and her friends to live in. Easy Bake Ovens, that sort of thing, because Mom got it, and she rolled her eyes when he'd give me whatever monstrosity he'd made in his workshop. He'd smile like a dope and I'd pretend to love it and we were bonded in the happy glue of that lie.

Those were better times.

The thing is, I've gotten rid of all the Barbies and the Easy Bake Oven is collecting dust in Mom's garage. But I've kept the things he made for me.

I speak to Mom regularly, and all I get from him are these fucking postcards.

And I actively resent Mom, but for him, it's a distant tingle, you know. And there's an ocean right beneath it, and...

And, well, I think you get the point. I hope Santa does whenever I bother to explain it to her.

But the thing is, I love her. So I think I should keep some parts of myself very far away.

Does that make sense?

That's what you do.

That's what you're supposed to do. Even when the missing is too much.

That's what Christmas is about, as far as I can tell, and I put away that postcard before it makes me cry.

On wobbly legs, I make my way back through the hole and into the bathroom. I discard the six pack's cardboard in the toilet trash, and put the bottles in the sink to be used as pins later. I'm collecting myself, preparing to leave, to return home to my crumbling couch, when I hear it.

Shuffling.

Somewhere in the bowling alley.

And then I hear laughter.

Snickering in the dark like giggle fits, and a cold spasm travels the length of my spine and coils around the beer in my stomach.

Someone else is in here with me.

Someone I don't know.

In this abandoned building, after midnight on Christmas.

And the thing is, it isn't just one someone. It's *someones*.

Because those hissing giggles are coming from different directions. Quiet, delighted escapes of air coming from the dark. Hushed amusement. I'm being watched.

Different pools of shadow, and I recognize how many holes in the ground there are here. How many hiding spots. How alone I am and surrounded in the dark, and for a moment, the panicking sensation is too much. I'm too frozen to scream.

Then one of the shadows starts to move. It bunches up into a ball, and rolls towards me, like an aggressive oil drop, only bigger than it should be. And it's as though a part of my mind snaps off and rolls clean down the inside of my head, behind my face, and when that worm of madness stops inside my mouth, I finally scream.

It does, too.

It stops in front of me, and the shadowy fur peels back to reveal sharp, white teeth. And it's screaming, waving its stumpy arms around like a lunatic, and then other oil drops are rolling out of the shadows, too. Rolling down the lanes towards me like bowling balls, peppered from the holes in the ground like black globs of snow all screaming and chattering. I'm too full of electric horror to make sense of it, and I run.

I run towards the front door, but they're there, too, rolling across the floor like prickly, inky tumbleweeds, with large, dry eyes from gray peeled back lids. Blinking and shrieking and rolling around.

I turn on a dime and head back towards the bathroom. I didn't put the ceiling tile back in place and shards of white moonlight shine down like God's hope, and I'm stepping on the sink again, reaching upwards, my panicked heart threatening to jack hammer right out of my chest and fall to the floor below. The little beasts, rolling down the hallway, gather beneath me as I hop up on the hand dryer and reach towards the hole in the ceiling.

A dull part of my brain recognizes that they aren't so black in the moonlight. Deep auburn, maybe. And sickly greens.

They're chattering still, giggling like hyenas, salivating all over the bathroom floor, leaving clean trails in the grime, and it must be a horrible combination of my fear and the beer, because it sounds like, "Ho, ho, ho!"

Ho, ho, ho, ho, ho, ho, ho

I pull up, immediately fall back on my butt, and I'm scrambling backwards, towards the edge, fearing they'll well up in the holes in the ceiling like bubbling oil springs. The pulsing of the blood in my ears grows louder and louder, louder and louder, until it's starting to sound like an engine, somewhere right above my head, ripping the night around me...

Only that's what it is. It is an engine. I look up and there's a sleek, metallic bullet oozing soft blue light from its under carriage being hauled across the sky by what look like armored deer. And they're coming closer. Closer and closer, and I realize they aim to land on the roof of The Missile.

I scramble backwards, until my right hand feels nothing, and I realize I'm backed up against the edge of the roof. I'm bound to fall right off if I scramble anymore, so instead I bunch my knees up against my chin and watch as the armored deer land on the rooftop beside me.

They don't move naturally. Their legs move in unison and there's a metal pole running through them, connecting them to the bullet with the blue lights, as though they're shish kebab'd and about as autonomous as life-sized foosball players. When they touch ground, their legs stop moving, and the engine begins to die.

Then there is silence. The mechanical reindeer pause. The top of the bullet springs back like a sleek trap door, and she steps out.

And I'm stunned.

She's trim, in a form-fitting red dress that might as well be painted on, with black stockings and boots like ashes and soot that crunch on the gravel of the rooftop when she touches the ground.

Her hair is black, cut short around her ears, and her skin is dark. A light-colored scar rips her face from the left corner of her mouth to somewhere south of her right eye, across a sharp nose. She bats her eyes and removes a cigar from her mouth, letting the smoke encircle her head like a wreath, the burning end twinkling like a cherry. And her eyes light on me. She twists her head, almost accusingly, and runs her finger along the side of her nose.

Then says, "Hola".

I feel as though I might pee myself as I see the auburn and green creatures pulling themselves up from the hole behind her.

"Ha visto a mis amigos?" she says, and her voice is smooth. Warm jelly, a bowl full of it, and I feel funny in the head. Funnier still when she smiles, and I realize I'm not intimidated but relaxed.

Warm and relaxed because I am peeing myself. She's polite enough not to stare.

"My friends," she says again. "Have you seen them?"

I start to speak, but it's babble that falls out of my lips, so instead I point behind her.

She turns her head as the first one cautiously makes its way towards her and then wraps its stubbly arms around her leg and hugs her. The rest follow behind, and those hysterical noises have gone. Now it's only a calm, bubbling murmur that passes from their teethy mouths.

"There you are!" she says, patting the first one on the head while the others stumble up towards her and hug different parts of her. "Mis mierdecillas," she says, grinning. Then she looks over at me.

"My little shits."

I laugh in spite of myself.

"I told them this year they could set off on their own as long as they stayed on the trail. As long as they stayed together. But you got yourselves a little lost, didn't you?" she says, peeling her eyes from me to the creatures around her. In the outside light, they are clearly red and green. All of them, like a shuffling parade of Christmas-colored puppy dogs walking towards her on their hind legs.

I laugh again. They're maybe cute and I've maybe lost my mind.

"It's okay," she says through that confident smile, then puffs again on her cigar. "You'll stay with me this time. We'll work on it, and maybe next time you can go off on your own. Okay?"

She turns to me again and shakes her head, that easy smile like magic on her lips.

"I'm sorry if they scared you," she says. "They don't mean to. You know who they are, don't you?"

The thing is, I do, but I can't say it. I still can't speak, even if I want to.

"*Elves*," she says, then shrugs sleepily. "A crude reduction of the actual name of their species. Great, great grandpa never really liked the term elves. He preferred the scientific name, but it's a mouthful and we've gotten easier with the times."

"Great g-grandpa?" I finally manage.

She smiles again, mischievous, and kind of shimmies, the way my mischievous Santa shimmied earlier. "You know who I'm talking about."

"Bullshit," I say. "And I'd like to wake up, please," but that comes out a giggle, too. I feel like I'm a child again. In my dad's workshop, surrounded by the warm drizzle of sawdust. Before the red looked like blood and more like Santa Claus and I thank whatever god made this possible.

She laughs, too. Chortles, and the smoke comes out in polite bursts. "Don't worry. It isn't all that. No naughty or nice or magic bullshit. All this is just a family affair, mostly. El negocio familiar. The old man was a scientist. And an explorer. Found these guys in a crater in the ice a long time ago. The money for the expedition was funded by guys who eventually funneled their wealth into Coca-Cola. And that," she says, sucking triumphantly on her cigar, "is how you know I'm not lying."

"I believe you," I whisper, and I realize I sort of have a crush on her. I also wish I hadn't peed myself in front of her. The little green and red elves are threading in and out of her legs now, hopping up and down with obvious excitement.

"So that makes you...?" I'm about to say Mrs. Claus, but then I think stubbornly, *That's my role*, and I figure I have lost my mind just a little bit. My New Year's resolution will be to drink less, because this is all just a bit too much.

"Mariana Claus," she says.

"Ms. Claus..."

She shrugs. "One of many. My sisters are fanned out all over right now, doing the same thing. Hopefully with more success than myself. We've been running this show for a while now. Since Mama passed away." She crosses herself then, the cigar clamped between her fingers and leaving a smoky residue in the air before her.

"This whole thing?" I ask. "You mean Christmas?"

She shrugs and chews on her lip. "Yeah. Sorta. It's more like these little guys here?" she says, and points at the grinning, giggling little elves by her feet. "They are the friendliest alien species we've ever been in contact with. We've got this big satellite dish up north, and we've talked to plenty, okay? That's what we do. Believe that or don't, but it's true."

"I do believe you!"

"You're way too easy," she says. "And pretty, too." I could die. I think maybe I do. She winks, then goes on. "Anyway, they love people. Human culture. They want to be friends. But they scare people, the way they look. I think they're cute, though." She says that, then drops to her knees, and one rushes up, right towards her face, with its teeth wide and glistening. For a moment my heart skips. It looks as though the little bastard might bite her face clean off. But a small, pink tongue comes up and laps at her cheek. She hands it the cigar. It puffs it, then falls backwards, and pretends to be dead. The other elves laugh, like helium popping. A bubbly, carbonated frenzy of shivering red and green bodies. And I'm laughing, too.

"Anyway," she says, prying the cigar from its fingers before it rolls away. "One way they've learned how to express themselves is to give gifts. It makes kids happy, makes them happy, and we get to try out new equipment. So we've done this for some time." She shrugs again, puffing on the cigar thoughtfully. "We try to stay in the dark, though. Don't want anyone to see, because we don't want anyone to…complicate their lives. They've got a good thing with us. We have a good thing with them. So don't tell anyone, okay?"

I nod.

"You promise?"

"Cross my heart."

"Good girl," she says. "You peed yourself," she says, and my heart drops.

"Yeah, I…"

"They scared you, yes?"

"Yes."

"It's okay. They know they scare people so they make them these."

She pulls out a present, wrapped in vibrant foil paper and tinsel. I stand shakily to my feet and she hands it to me. Then the elves pile around her, some on her shoulders, one perched on her head, all staring eagerly with excitement. They're nervous with anticipation. You could hear a pin drop, they're so eager to see me open the present. So I do.

I tear back the paper.

It's a macaroni frame. The paper says, "From Santa" in chicken scratch, and it reminds me of my dad, and I miss him all the same.

"I love it," I say, and they begin to cheer and stomp around, and two of them rush right towards me. I feel my heart drop again, but then they're hugging my legs, the way they hugged hers.

"You see? It lights up the world just a little bit," she says, sucking once more on her cigar, the end of it simmering like burning red honey. "So they make little homemade gifts like that and we pass 'em out wherever we can. Kids usually think those are the ones from their parents. But Mom and Dad generally get the big stuff. Less personal. We work on a budget, you know, and everything these little guys do is from the heart."

I hold it against my chest, imagine filling the frame and hanging it above my couch, and I feel something bubbling inside and turning into goosebumps on my skin.

"I see that you're alone tonight," she says, squinting as she drags on her cigar. "But it's harder to feel like everyone's missing when you can feel the love immediately around you, right? Hugging the hell out of your legs, yes?"

I laugh, and those popping helium sounds of laughter fill the air again.

"So that's their gift. I hope you like it."

"I love it," I say.

"All right, mis mierdecillas! Let's ride!"

I watch them scurry away, piling into that silver bullet, and then she's standing on top of it, preparing to drop back inside, when she turns to me with a wink. "Happy Holidays," she purrs, smiling self-consciously.

"You too!" I say.

"And to all a good night," she says, before sliding easily into the bullet.

I whisper something back. I'm clutching that frame to my chest as the engine starts up again. As those robotic reindeer begin pumping their legs, as the blue light fans out from beneath the bullet. It rises from the rooftop, and is gone just as quickly as it came.

Almost as if it was never there at all.

I put a picture of me and my parents in the macaroni frame. I crop it so Dad's right arm is out of the picture, like I think he'd want. I dunno. I think it would make him happy. I'd like to see him how he sees himself. Without the shame, without the guilt, if that's possible. I know I might never see him again, which is ugly and sad, but maybe it's okay. Maybe he's got a frame just like this somewhere. Maybe he's missing me the way I'm missing him. That feels real to me, even if it probably isn't.

I cut and paste a picture of my little Santa Claus in there, too. In the corner. It's crude and funny, but it works. It's family.

She's family.

And that's all I've got.

Another brief, sharp pain shoots through my foot, like licks of fire, that have been coming and going from my bum toe.

It hurts when the nerves start to feel again.

Anyway, I can't wait to tell my girlfriend all about it and I hope she comes home to my shitty couch soon. So I can show her this silly picture and beg for her to stay a part of my silly life.

To be a part of my silly family.

I hope she likes it, being part of my family. I hope she wants to be there, too.

I'll call her tonight and tell her I miss her. So she can hear my voice and I can hear hers.

Absence, they say, makes the heart grow fonder.

As I spend another Christmas alone, I guess I'm finding out all the time that that's true.

UNEXPECTED GUESTS
Andrew Wilson

Elora, Lady of the Winter Twilight, cupped her hand to gather snow as it fell. She gently formed a ball with the flakes, then held the white sphere at eye level.

"Is that for me?" Her husband stood an arm's length away with a smile on his face. His red suit, styled to match current human fashion trends, stood out against the dark blues and grays of their castle home.

"Must you make that joke every year?" Elora rolled her eyes and tossed the snowball into the center of the courtyard, where it exploded in a shower of glittering crystals. Sparks flew between the crystalline motes, forming the gate from the flurry of ice and lightning. Elora waved a hand, channeling a bit of her will into the ground beneath the gate. The snow and soil, indeed the very fabric of reality in the twilight world of her people, eagerly responded to her commands. Icy pillars grew from the snow-covered ground and arched over the gate.

Nikolaos scratched his beard. There was little besides white in it, a sharp contrast to his dark skin. "I do not have many visits left, my love. I was not a young man when you found me, and a handful of days adds up after fourteen centuries."

"And have you chosen?" Elora asked. "Will you leave one year and never return, or will you stay with me? I fear one year you will simply die upon stepping through the gate."

"God has not yet sent me a clear sign to choose one or the other." He chuckled. "Perhaps I shall simply flip a coin, as they say?"

Elora rolled her eyes again and gently shoved her husband toward the gate. "Go, Nikolaos. Drink deep of the mortal world, then return to me."

Nikolaos cupped Elora's cheek, a twinkle in his eye, then turned and stepped through the gate. He vanished in a shower of sparks and ice crystals. Elora raised her hand and twisted her wrist. Spines of ice grew from the gate's pillars and wrapped around the swirling energy cloud, to guard from within and without until her beloved returned.

#

Elora set down her book as a foul shiver burned across her skin. Snow and ice shook from her library's windows as the realm itself shuddered in pain. She hissed as a second burn erupted across her senses.

Iron. The word flared in her mind as she stood. *Someone brought iron here.*

Elora summoned her armor with a thought. Tendrils of snow flowed through the air and gathered around her body, and metal-hard plates of ice formed around her limbs as she pushed through the great doors in her hall. The guardians on either side of the doors looked down at her for direction. Her creations loomed head and shoulders above her, wrought of stone and ice. Their presence was a comfort, but they were just as vulnerable to iron as she, and far slower.

"Watch," she commanded. "Let no one enter the hall, or the courtyard."

The guardians nodded, their armor-like bodies scraping like stone rubbing on metal. She passed two more sets of the stone figures on the way out, and repeated her commands, then shut and sealed the doors with a wave of her hand, and bounded into the eternal twilight.

The first site of iron contamination in the snow covered forests of Elora's home was marked by an angry, red wound. She crouched beside it, her hand hovering above the molten slag.

Her realm was a living thing, and would recover. The iron, provided it was not too heavy or large, would be encapsulated and isolated, like an oyster creating a pearl.

This specific contamination resembled a blade of some sort. A small, unbalanced dagger, with a serrated edge. Too thin to be a proper weapon.

A frustrated snarl ripped from Elora's throat as she recognized the blade. It was not intended to be a weapon at all; it was a table knife, like might be found in any kitchen in the human world.

Elora dashed through the woods to the second wound. The trees passed in a blur until she arrived at a second molten circle around an identical steak knife.

A third wound shivered across the realm, and Elora snarled and dashed toward the new incursion. Now she would catch the intruders in the act. They were obviously mortals, and could not expect her to arrive so quickly after they dropped their forbidden iron.

A burning brand lashed across Elora's shins and sent her tumbling to the ground. The third wound blazed in front of her face as she skidded across the snow, and an iron net dropped from the trees. Elora screamed as the wires dug into her skin. Her strength, her power, her connection to the realm itself, fled from the iron. Only when consciousness also fled did the pain fade.

Voices trickled in through the darkness, while Elora grappled with the spider's web of pain and fire that bound her skin. After a moment, the web withdrew from her skin, but lingered nearby, a pulsing wound on her lands. The touch of iron remained around her wrists, though. Manacles, a distant part of her mind identified.

"How long before she wakes up?" A deep voice rumbled through the darkness. "Kelsey, you're the expert."

"Careful with names," a female snapped. "Why did you use that net? You said this would be in and out, no one hurt. She's one of the Great Lords. Do you know how bad it is to anger one of them?"

"No one's been hurt," the man replied. "See, she's already healing. How long before she wakes up?"

"I think she *is* awake," another man said, his voice squeaked with anxiety. "Her ears twitched."

"Good," the first man growled. His boots shuffled on the carpet as he moved closer. Elora hissed as the man grabbed her ear and yanked her head to one side. "This is the home of Claus, right? Where's the treasure, bitch? "

Shadows and stars, another of those. Every few years she encountered treasure hunters who pieced together old fairy stories with modern myths and arrived at the conclusion her home must be some mystic treasure storehouse. She sucked in a breath and forced her voice to stay level. "This is not the Wild Hunt's grounds, though I'm sure Wodan will not give you much of a welcome."

The first man released her ear and stood with a wordless snarl. "We'll do this the hard way, then. Kelsey, keep her bound. Wilks, with me."

Elora cracked her eyes, and saw the blurry forms of two men stomp out of the library. The woman, Kelsey, sat on her heels an arms length away, her fingers clenching the hilt of a dagger in a white-knuckled death grip. Her face was a mix of anger and fear that, in Elora's experience, led to either great or horrible actions.

"Who had the notion to use iron?" Elora coughed as her throat protested so many words.

"Please don't talk to me," Kelsey whispered. "This wasn't supposed to happen. Taylor and Wilks weren't supposed to cause any damage."

"And you believed them," Elora snarled.

Kelsey flinched, the dagger's hilt squeaked as her grip tightened. "I'm sorry. I don't know what they're thinking. I've been trapped here for...months? Longer? They came through another gate, but it was one-way, and we needed yours to get out. I was able to guide them here, but—"

"They cannot control the gate," Elora snarled. "If you release me now, I will spare you and allow you to return to the human world."

"I need your word that—"

"Now!" Elora clenched her fists, wishing she could summon her armor through the cursed iron. "Safe passage, or, if you do not act, you will suffer their fates. That I swear!"

Kelsey took a slow breath, slid her dagger into a padded sheath at her belt, then quickly undid the manacles. Elora slid out of the iron with a sigh. The angry welts faded from her wrists. Each breath reconnected her with her realm, bringing strength. She could feel the two intruders stomping through the fortress in a vain search for some fabled treasure room, their iron weapons radiating corruption and pain.

"You are not carrying iron," Elora whispered.

Kelsey shook her head. "Silver and bronze. I didn't think they would be so stupid and cruel and I was so desperate to get home."

"They're human," Elora spat. She stood and stretched. She eyed the woman. So easy to kill her, now that her power was returning. No, that would not do. She'd pledged that one safe passage, and to break her word would destroy her realm. It could survive a thousand thousand iron infections, but would die the instant she broke her word. "The number of your kind that are not needlessly cruel was few even before you overran the Earth."

Kelsey straightened and met Elora's glare with a stubborn gaze. "The same could be said of your people, Lady."

Perhaps there is hope for this one, yet. Elora's lips twitched in an involuntary smile. "Which of my cousins wronged you so?"

"He's dead," Kelsey snapped, "so it doesn't matter any more. Dead with my only iron through his heart, and my daughter home. But the gate out of his realm closed before I could escape."

"It is a shame that such an accusation does not narrow down who caused the offense," Elora muttered. "Gather up that net. Do not let it touch anything. The central courtyard has the gate you seek. Go now, and I will open it for you when I deal with the others. My guardians will let you pass."

Kelsey shook her head. "Wilks has something. He took control of some, destroyed others."

Elora paused, and reached out. The human spoke true. She could not feel her guardians. Normally they were a quiet rumble in the back of her mind, easily ignored after they were given instructions. Now, the rumble was muted, as though behind a wall or curtain. She reached for them, but they did not respond to her power.

"Bother," Elora spat as she summoned her armor anew.

Elora prowled through the corridors underneath her fortress. The mortar between the stones glowed with cold, blue light, letting her see the damage the humans had done. She followed the trail of broken locks and hanging doors through the corridors. Each door she passed tore her heart. These were the rooms where Nikolaos stored his souvenirs from Earth, centuries of clothing, books, artwork were contained within. Such would be all she would have of him for however long she lived after he eventually died.

Such short lives. Elora shook her head. Nikolaos would live or die as a human, with that human heart she fell in love with centuries before. But she would not allow his legacy to be defiled by thieves.

Two guardians stood at a cross corridor. The stone and metal constructs turned as one and faced her. She raised her hands and pushed against them with her will. Frost rimed the joints of the armored figures and they slowed. The layer of frost solidified into a coating of ice, freezing both in place. Elora stepped forward, placed a hand on one helm-like head, and pushed her will into the guardian.

Her will slid off the guardian's core and she frowned. The piece of herself she had put into the stone figures so long ago remained within, but it had been severed from her control. She shifted her concentration to the chest. The material of the guardian's construction parted under her hand, allowing her to reach into the cavity and remove the fragment of power. She crushed the core, and felt the fragment of power rejoin the whole of her with a shiver. The guardian crumbled to the floor in a pile of rubble.

The other guardian's arm shattered the ice that restrained it and slammed into her side. Her breath blew out as she struck the wall. Elora ducked under a second blow and plunged her fist into the guardian's chest. The stone parted under her blow like paper, and the construct tumbled lifeless to the floor a moment later.

Taylor stepped out of a storeroom. He brandished his iron dagger, keeping the cursed blade between his body and Elora. "You make a lot of noise, lady."

"You came into my home as a thief," Elora snarled, "and you expect courtesy?"

"We just want the treasure," Taylor replied. "And then we will leave your realm in peace."

"Treasure?" Elora laughed. The sharp, musical notes echoed through the stone corridors, even as pain in her side from the guardian's blow grew. She brought up her hand and let her power flow into her palm to create a ball of light. "You knew enough to come here, yet you still think he's the saint, or Father Christmas? Foolish."

"We researched it," Wilkes said as he cowered in the doorway. "Years of research. Found the pattern he followed, predicted when and where he would be. We found a path through three other realms to get here!"

Taylor raised his blade and pointed at Elora's face. "It'll be worth it. No piles of gold or gems, but all that art? All those little bits and pieces he's collected over the centuries? We'll be rich, Wilkes."

Elora's smile grew as she closed her fist. The ball of light transformed into a bar of frozen lightning that hissed as she brought it around into a ready stance. "My husband loves to travel, to visit new places every year. And ever since he visited England, he's been confused with the saint, Woden, and others."

"It's over." Wilkes surged to his feet and jabbed Taylor in the chest. "We can't get out through her, she—"

Taylor fixed Elora with a glare, then swung Wilkes around and shoved him toward her. Elora raised her blade, but the flash of Nikolaus' face in her mind's eye stayed her hand. She drove an elbow into Wilkes' belly, and sent him to the ground with a sweep of her leg. Her blade she kept pointed at Taylor. The larger man narrowed his eyes as his companion whimpered on the ground.

"I expected you to kill him."

Elora shrugged. "My husband's brand of mercy is infectious. Surrender and you both shall live. You will labor until the damage you have done to my realm is repaired, but you will live, and you will eventually return to the mortal world."

"No deal." Taylor snarled and leapt at Elora. She sidestepped the clumsy thrust and drove her blade through his chest. The human's face froze in an expression of disbelief as frost spread from his breastbone. Fingers of ice wrapped around his body, coating him in a layer of white crystals.

Elora let her blade dissipate with a final hiss.

Kelsey eyed the gate with suspicion. "Where will it take me?"

Elora shrugged. "I cannot say. Nikolaos wished to see the world, and I crafted the gate to meet his needs. You will emerge near a large population center, where a language you know is spoken."

Kelsey's suspicious gaze turned to Elora. "With respect, Lady Elora, the definition of 'large' has changed since you created the gate. And how many languages does your husband know?"

"Currently spoken or in total?" Elora shook her head. She found herself disappointed that the human woman was leaving. While their meeting had been less than auspicious, the days since had demonstrated the young woman's considerable wit. A pleasant change from the normal human thieves that occasionally stumble through the natural gates. Even more pleasant than her own boorish kin. "It matters not. Nor that perception has changed. The gate adapts. You will not be stranded, child."

Kelsey nodded, and adjusted the pack on her shoulders which contained all the iron that Kelsey and her companions had brought into Elora's realm. Even through the protective cover, it pulsed like Elora's still-healing bruises from the guardian's blow.

Wilkes trudged through the snow to the gate. His legs were coated in a thin layer of stone, binding him to the fabric of the realm. Kelsey glanced at him, then shuddered.

"What will happen to Taylor's body?"

Elora waved a hand to the trees beyond the fortress' walls. "His shell already feeds the forest you three injured. I have a final request for you to repay your debt to me and my realm."

Kelsey eyed the gate, then looked back to Elora. "What is your request?"

Elora snapped her fingers, and let the bindings protecting the gate fall away. "You know my people and our lands. I imagine you will be sought out for advice. Should any attempt to link my realm to Father Christmas, the saint, Woden, or even Krampus, discourage them."

"I will." Kelsey nodded, then her eyes narrowed. "Wait, Krampus is real?"

"Not my tale to tell." Elora turned to the gate, but before she could nudge Kelsey through, it flared and a figure made of light stepped through.

Elora summoned her blade. The silhouette had the look of a man, but made of bright, golden light, which sloughed off it like water. A white-haired man in a red suit shook his head and smiled at Elora.

"Ho!" Nikolaos called as he stepped through. "Blessed evening to you, my love."

"Nikolaos," Elora smiled and slipped an arm around her husband's shoulder. "Welcome home."

"My lady love." Nikolaos pointed to Kelsey. "Who are these? Visitors? Or uninvited guests?"

"A stray," Elora replied with a gesture to Kelsey. "Trapped on this side of the gate. I was allowing her to go home."

"That is generous of you. Perhaps I am a good influence on your soul." Nikolaos grinned like a mischievous boy. "And our new servant?"

"Less welcome, and indebted."

Nikolaos frowned, then shook his head. "How bad?"

Kelsey bowed. "Sir, I—"

Nikolaos raised a hand to silence her. "I think it is time for you to depart, young lady. I have lived on this side of the gate long enough to know the effects of iron, and the sooner your bag is away, the better."

Kelsey glanced at Elora, received a nod, and hurled herself through the gate. Her form was consumed by a golden glow an instant before touching the gate itself. Her glowing figure melted into the light of the gate, before it faded into a cloud of motes.

Nikolaos nodded, "Now, perhaps I should hear your tale of the past few days."

Elora smiled and led her husband inside. Her new servant trudged behind them.

THE TRUE STORY OF CHRISTINA AND KRISTOPHER KRINGLE

Revealed Without Permission
Ross Van Dusen

No one could remember when the Lovings and their daughter, Christina, moved in. They were just there one day—weren't they? Had they always been there? Regardless, all his life, as far as he could remember, Kristopher had lived two doors down from Christina—he was almost the boy next door.

When walking to school together, if they bumped shoulders or arms, there would be a spark. "It's just static," Christina would say (although she knew differently), and Kristopher believed her. *Why wouldn't he?*

They lived by the Wood—what everyone called the forest that nearly surrounded the town—and played hide-and-seek, catch the rabbit (their name for tag), and king of the trees.

Playing rabbit, no one could catch Tina, and when it came to hide-and-seek she always—magically—found everyone. Kris was okay with that. It helped that he always won king of the trees. He would climb the highest and yell, "I'm on top of the world."

When they played in the Wood, they never ventured in very far—

there was a rumor, kind of a scary rumor, that strange things lived in the back of the Wood, where the trees thinned and the snow never melted.

That far north, even in the summer, there was enough snow in town to make a snowball and take aim at old Mr. Goochy's top hat. Mr. Goochy would growl and shake his fist, but everyone knew he didn't really mean it. His hat was held on with a cord, so the most any kid could hope for was to knock it down over his eyes, which would bring an even louder growl from Mr. Goochy and fits of laughter from the children. Within a block, however, a smile could be seen on Mr. Goochy's face—*if anyone was looking, that is.*

Fall and winter were snow forts and snowball battles for every kid in town. Tina was the most accurate. Even if you were hidden behind a three-foot snow-fort wall, she could throw a curveball that would drop in and hit you right on top of your head. She wouldn't have missed Mr. Goochy's top hat, that's for sure, but Kris noticed she never took aim at it. He never said anything, he just noticed.

In high school, when Kris offered to carry Tina's books, she wouldn't let him. He was okay with that. And though he was no slouch, Kris's grades were never as high as Tina's, but he was okay with that, too. Just as in running, no one could keep up with Tina.

Then one day, on the way to school, Tina took Kris's hands, and he felt an electrical surge. Not like the spark they'd felt from the occasional bump or touch, not like that at all. When she took his hands, Kris felt something tingly, yet numbing, and unexplainably pleasant. Tina smiled, "Did you feel that?" she asked.

Kris felt it all right, right down to his toes. He felt it so strongly he was speechless. "Yes," he finally muttered.

"Good," she answered and smiled knowingly.

Kris never felt the same after Tina took his hands. From that day on, high school was wonderful. School, and holding hands, and seeing Tina in class, was wonderful.

His senior year, Kris worked part-time in his father's woodshop, making banisters and custom turnings for the hardware store. Got pretty good at it, too.

Meanwhile Tina helped keep the books and manage her father's business—a business that no one in town really understood. But, *whatever* it was, she was great at managing it.

Tina's perfect grades earned her a four-year scholarship in business and logistics at Oxford in far off England.

Kris knew he would be heartbroken without her but when Christina left, she said, "Don't worry, Kris, things will work out, you wait and see." She kissed him, took his hands, and held them longer and stronger than ever before. Then she waved goodbye.

Every time Tina had kissed Kris he'd felt stronger, or safer—or somehow—or something—or somewhat—he didn't know what. That last kiss, that tender kiss, and her holding his hands, both of his hands, was even more of—he didn't know what.

While Tina was gone, Kris did his woodwork beautifully. Except, he was fidgety, very fidgety. His father finally said, "Why don't you put all that fidgety energy to good use? Make something."

Kris started making toys. He soon made the best toys in the land and then gave them to the children in town. When his father suggested he sell them instead of giving them away, Kris said, "I make enough money in the woodshop turning banisters and such. Besides, I like to see the look on the kids' faces when I give them my toys—it takes my mind off Tina." Kris thoughtfully stopped. "Or…maybe, it makes me think of her more…and feel much better."

Well, there was no arguing with logic like that.

After four years, Tina came home a highly educated, logistical whizz. Kris was overjoyed to see her. "Look at all the toys I've made," he said.

"I knew you would," she answered.

Tina looked into his eyes, took his hands, and held them for a very long time. Kris didn't exactly understand, yet somehow he knew. He didn't exactly know what he knew, but he knew that he knew it.

Kris didn't know what to do next, so he just held her hands, looked into her amazingly beautiful brown eyes, and waited.

"It's time for us to make a life together, Kris," she finally said.

"Yes! Yes! Marry me, Tina. Marry me, and we can have a wonderful life and grow old together."

"I will marry you," Tina said with a knowing smile, "And we'll grow older, Kris, but we're never going to grow old."

"We're getting married, and we're never growing old? How does that work?" Kris was only somewhat mystified—Tina had never been wrong about anything. At least not that Kris had ever known or seen.

"It's too hard to explain. You'll get the gist of it after we're married."

And Kris was okay with that.

Within a month they were married in the little town church. Everyone in the little town watched as Tina and Kris became Christina and Kristopher Kringle. They waved goodbye under a shower of birdseed, rice, and confetti. (It seems some of the townspeople were ecologists, some were not, and some just liked to party.)

As they rode their sleigh out of town, Tina said, "Turn here."

Kris was a little surprised. "Into the Wood? Are you sure? They say that strange things live back in the Wood. No one ever goes there."

"Yes, I know. There's a place back there for us. I thought it best to show you rather than try to describe it to you." Tina touched Kris's hand once more, and he felt a surge of confidence.

Off they went, into the Wood, deeper and deeper, into thicker and thicker forest. The forest seemed to open just enough to let the sleigh through. Kris didn't notice the trees and shrubs magically closing after they passed.

"Are you sure about this, Tina?"

Tina smiled and said, "Yes, I'm sure."

Suddenly, to Kris's surprise the Wood started to thin, soon becoming only a few trees scattered here and there. Then barely any trees at all. "Well, what do you know? I thought the Wood went on forever."

Tina smiled her knowing smile, then she pointed. "Do you see that little cabin in the distance? Head for that."

"Is that our little love nest?" Kris asked, "It doesn't seem very big."

"You'll make it bigger," Tina said.

"All by myself? I don't think so!" Kris was more than a little skeptical.

"We'll have all the help we'll need," she said with assurance.

Kris pulled the sleigh up in front of the cabin. Tina jumped down and opened the door. "Come on, slowpoke. Come meet your new helpers."

She stamped the snow off her boots and waved Kris in. Confused but willing, Kris climbed off the sleigh and entered through the little door. He stood paralyzed. An army of little men and women started clapping and cheering. Tina was so happy she had tears in her eyes.

"You have a special gift, Kristopher. I knew you were the one, the first time I took your hands."

"The one? The one what?" Kris asked.

"The one to bring joy to the children in the world."

"Oh really? And how am I supposed to do that?" he asked.

"The toys you made for the children in town? You gave them to the children to see the joy in their faces, isn't that right?"

"Yes, of course, but—"

"Well, now you can make toys for many more children—for children everywhere. These men will be your helpers."

"But, but this place is so small, Tina! My helpers, and you, and myself practically fill the entire cabin."

"Well then, the first thing you and your helpers will need to do is build a bigger workshop, isn't it?" Tina brought in their belongings and started unpacking. "Well, get started," she commanded. "Spring is on the way and fall and winter will be on us before you know it."

Bewildered, Kris started by asking his little men to start cutting

123

timber for a bigger workshop. They were on the task faster than even Tina could have imagined. Tools magically appeared, and trees from the edge of the forest fell like dominoes. Lumber piled up to the height of the windows, and the ground was prepared before nightfall.

Tina and her little women had prepared a supper. Kris sat with her at the head of the table eating a fine stew of rabbit and potatoes and carrots while their army of helpers filled the rest of the table, jabbering and celebrating the day's efforts. Tina looked pleased, and that was good enough for Kris.

Breakfast appeared as magically as had supper. Kris whispered to Tina. "How is all this happening, Tina? I mean, it's wonderful and all, but holy cow! You know what I mean?"

Tina smiled. "It is wonderful." Then she touched his hands and said, "You have work to do. So go now...and do."

Every time Tina touched him, he felt stronger. Kris jumped up, and his helpers jumped up as well. The walls of his new workshop started to grow. By noon the walls were above the heads of his little helpers. Only Kris could see over them. By nightfall the roof beams were in.

"Supper!" Tina called. The work stopped and the little men poured in through the back window, tumbling and stumbling to get to the table. "Tomorrow you'll make that into a proper door," she announced. Kris's answer was a nod and a laugh.

Within days the roof was on, and the massive workshop was buttoned up. Tables and workspaces were laid out. Tina had sent for a wagonload of supplies. She met the shipment at the edge of the trees and brought the wagon through the forest herself.

Kris set about making the toys he so loved to make. His little men learned from him and soon matched his skill. "My helpers are fast learners," he said to Tina, holding up two identical, beautifully assembled, perfectly painted dolls. "I can't tell mine from theirs'."

"Let's call them elves," she responded.

"The dolls?" Kris looked confused.

"Your helpers are elves," she explained. "They're very much like people...but not."

"Not what?" Kris was still confused.

"Not people. They're elves."

"Oh...okay." As they would say in the rest of the world, Kris Kringle had learned to roll with the punches. His world, this world that Tina had brought him into, this world he came to understand, wasn't anything like the rest of the world. And he was okay with that.

As the spring surrendered to summer, the giant workshop started filling with toys. By fall the shelves were full, and many more toys were stacked on the floor. It was the best year of Kristopher's life. He was making all kinds of toys, the best he'd ever made.

Christina was by his side, watching over the whole operation like an invisible general. She would scan the operation, disappear into the office every once in a while and somehow there would be enough wood and cloth and stuffing and metal and paint and plastic and wire and batteries to finish whatever Kris and his elves were working on.

Yet, there was something in the back of Kris's mind that kept pushing forward. Finally, as December came upon them, he asked Tina, "How am I going to deliver all these toys to all the children, Tina?"

Tina said with a twinkle in her eye, "We have a surprise for you, Kris." She led him around to the back of the massive workshop. Again, he was stunned. A stable had magically appeared. It contained eight tiny reindeer, quietly feeding on hay, and parked in its entrance was a sleigh. A bright-red, super-shiny, golden-trimmed sleigh. With its glistening silver runners, it was the most beautiful sleigh Kris Kringle had ever seen. "Where did this come from?" he finally asked.

"The elves and I decided to surprise you. This is how you're going to deliver all the toys," she beamed, "Isn't it wonderful?" The elves were giggling and congratulating themselves on their complete surprise.

"Yes...but...but...the reindeer...they're so small!" Kris protested.

"And the sleigh—that beautiful sleigh, is so big! How is this going to work?"

"Small reindeer can fly—large reindeer can't," was Tina's answer.

"We're going to fly!" he shouted.

"Much faster than using roads," she answered.

A bewildered Kris said, "Oh...okay." Suddenly he bolted up. "Hey! I don't know *how* to fly! I've never flown in my life. How am I supposed—"

"The reindeer know the way." Tina said. "You just announce a name; they'll take you to that child's roof."

"The roof? Why the roof? I'm not crazy about slippery roofs. Especially snow-covered slippery roofs."

"We figured that out, too. We have special boots for you so you won't slip. Landing on roofs and taking off again will be much faster. Plus, roofs are easier to land on than the ground—there are no trees in the way."

Resigned, Kris said, "Oh...okay." Then he raised a finger. "Ahh, how do I get the toys to the children? Do I leave them on the roof?"

"You slip down the chimney—put them in the room and zip back up. And on to the next roof—quick as a flash."

"Won't I get awfully sooty sliding down all those chimneys?"

"I've made a special suit for you." She showed Kris a bright red suit trimmed with white fur. "The soot won't stick to this specially treated suit. It's something I learned from the Scottish. The Scotts guard everything this way."

Kris's head was spinning. "When do I start? I should be getting started, shouldn't I? I mean...there *are* an awful lot of roofs."

Tina smiled. "We talked it over. You're going to deliver all the presents on Christmas Eve—when everyone's sleeping. Christmas morning will be the happiest surprise of all."

"Nobody talked to me about it—I didn't talk it over," Kris said in a daze.

"Do you trust me?" Tina asked.

Kris nodded his head. "How could I not? This has been the best year of my life. I didn't know I could feel this much joy—ever. It's been magical."

"Well...a little magic, maybe." Tina winked. "In truth, your hard work and skill are what made all the toys, isn't that right?"

"I guess, but delivering them all in one night? That's going to take some kind of...super magic!"

"You let me worry about that," Christina said, as she had said to him many times. "I'm finishing up a list. You can check the list over during the next few days to make sure everything's in order."

"Sure...okay." Kris returned to the cabin in a trance. The next morning he checked out the window to see if he'd been dreaming. The stable was still there—and the reindeer—and the beautiful sleigh.

It wasn't a dream.

It started to dawn on Kris how wonderful Christmas would be for the children. Over the next few days, Tina was very busy making the list. Kris checked it twice to make sure there were no mistakes. It was spot on. Not a problem on any one of the hundreds of pages.

Kris was really looking forward to flying. As the days passed and the time got closer, he grew more and more excited.

The night before the night of Christmas Eve, Kris was so excited he couldn't sleep. Tina slipped into bed next to him, saw his wide-open eyes, smiled, and kissed him on the forehead. "Sleep now," she said, and Kris relaxed. He was asleep in minutes. "Just a little magic," she whispered and went to sleep herself.

Christmas Eve day was spent loading the sleigh, while Kris paced, checked the list, and paced some more.

When the sleigh was fully loaded, Tina pinned a lock of her hair inside his jacket collar and said, "Okay, Kris, you're up!" *She hadn't intended a pun, but there it was.* Kris Kringle climbed aboard his shiny-red, golden-trimmed, silver-runnered, magnificent sleigh, tucked his list safely away, took a deep breath, saluted his elves, blew a kiss to his magical wife, Christina, snapped the reins, and took off.

Everyone cheered and waved. A joyous "Whoo, hoo-hooo!" could be heard as Kris flew into that crisp, moonlit, starry night.

"Do you think he'll be okay?" one of the elves asked Christina.

"Oh, yes," she said, "He'll be fine. I'm up there with him."

As time passed, all the young people moved away, and the little town eventually disappeared. After that, no one was exactly sure where the town had been or if it had ever been there at all.

The impenetrable forest remained unchanged, the trees seeming never to grow old.

Even now, as explorers trek all through the frozen tundra, and airplanes fly over the area almost every day, no one has ever spotted the little house with the giant workshop attached to it.

Over the years, Kris came to be known by many names—Father Christmas. St. Nicholas. Even Santa Clause.

Eventually his "Whoo, hoo-hooo!" came to be described as more of a "Ho, ho, ho."

And to this day, Christina Kringle has kept her promise to Kristopher—they've grown older, but magically, they've never grown old.

SHOULDERING THE BURDEN
M.L.D. Curelas

Phaedra stood on the deck of the *Northern Queen*. The salt-heavy air tickled her nose, and she sighed with contentment. It had been a long time since she'd been to Greece, her homeland. She'd accepted the special gift-bearer assignment as an excuse for a visit—and to banish her nightmares.

The dock workers called to them, and Phaedra answered. Then she translated the Greek instructions into Dutch for the elves, who quickly complied with the docking directions.

Since it was night, the elves hadn't bothered with glamors to hide pointed ear-tips or to add inches to their height. As the airship bumped gently into its docking berth, the elves slithered over the side and clambered down the ropes, securing the *Northern Queen* to the spindly dock that extended from the Piraeus Airship Tower.

Despite the commotion, the sobbing persisted. Incessant, heavy sobbing. Phaedra heard it every night, awake or asleep. It haunted her during the day, a ringing in her ears that never faded.

Catching sight of the customs agent, Phaedra summoned a welcoming smile. The official came aboard, navigating the gangplank with ease, and Phaedra felt a twinge of guilt for the lies she'd have to tell him—he seemed pleasant, if tired.

"*Kalí chroniá!*" she said warmly. It was New Year's Eve, and a wish for a good year was more appropriate than Merry Christmas, even if she was on a gift-bearing mission.

He blinked. "But you speak Greek so well! Surely, you are a daughter of our fair country."

His voice lilted, not quite a question, and Phaedra didn't wonder at his doubt. Even in the night, the elves' fair complexions and hair were striking. They darted around the deck of the airship like will o' the wisps. She smiled and beckoned the customs agent closer to one of the gas lamps.

"My husband and I live in the North now, so our airship is crewed with sailors from that land, but I am Greek, yes. How kind of you to not remark on my rusty words!" Phaedra laughed and touched his arm.

He relaxed. In the light, her bronze skin and dark eyes were arresting. Her wavy black hair, shot with strands of iron-gray and pinned up in a complicated knot, and her dress, high quality wool, spoke of a genteel woman of means.

"How wonderful to have you back home, then," he said with a smile. "You understand I need to see your manifest and travel log?"

"Of course," Phaedra said, "I have them here." She handed him the ledger.

"Oh…" The customs agent frowned. "You were in England?"

Phaedra kept her smile firmly in place. "Yes, shopping. I couldn't come home without gifts!"

"Of course, of course, but there was a theft from the museum there." He gave her an apologetic shrug. "We are supposed to search all ships coming from England. They've put out an alert all over the continent."

"Of course," Phaedra said. "What a shame you must stay late tonight, when your family must be waiting for the New Year to come. The *Northern Queen* is quite large."

He shifted his weight, tapping the ledger with nervous fingers. "Er...yes." He stared at her, the Greek woman with a stout, matronly figure and a warm smile, and cleared his throat. "Well, I'm sure everything is in order here. Why waste our time searching the ship of a daughter of Greece?" He signed her travel record and handed the ledger back to her.

As he disembarked, he turned, waved, and wished her a Happy New Year.

"Any sign of pursuit from England?"

Phaedra gasped and clutched her chest. Heart pounding, she swiveled. "Annika, you startled me!"

Annika bowed. "I'm sorry, Mrs. Claus, I thought you heard me approach." The elf folded her arms. "This gift-delivery would be easier if we used the sleigh. Its magic is stronger than the airship's."

Phaedra sighed. "This is Ágios Vassílis' night, and we're here with his permission. He's allowed us an airship, but no sleigh and no reindeer. That's not how it's done in Greece."

She and Nicholas had offered to give the statue to Vassílis for him to deliver, but he'd declined. He believed Phaedra, the only one who could hear the crying, should have the honor of delivery.

"We're taking the runabout to the Acropolis, Annika. It's so tiny that it's less likely to be noticed and it'll feel more...sleigh-like."

The elf snorted. "It will be slow and clumsy."

At that moment, half a dozen elves came up from belowdecks, carrying an oil-cloth swathed object. The marble statue was heavy, and the elves grunted and muttered. Phaedra did not speak Elvish but, judging by the scandalized look on Annika's face, suspected a few not-so-jolly words were dropping from their tongues.

"To answer your earlier question, there's no sign of any pursuit. They've discovered the theft, though. The customs agent had instructions to search for it."

Annika nodded. "We'll leave once it's loaded then?" She patted the leather satchel slung over her shoulder. "I am ready, are you?"

Phaedra smiled, indicating her dress—dark green with holly leaves and berries embroidered around the cuffs and hem—with a flourish. While most of her responsibilities at the North Pole involved managing the compound, the image of the gift-bearer was important. Useful tools, not important to the image, but good to have around, were discreetly tucked away—a collapsed telescoping parasol in one boot and a multi-tool in a pocket.

"Hmm," Annika said. "You're missing something." She reached into her satchel and pulled out a red velvet cloak trimmed with white rabbit fur.

"It's warm enough, I didn't think I'd need it, but you're right." Phaedra wrapped the cloak around her shoulders and fastened the clasp. "Should we bring Muninn, do you think?"

Annika grinned. "Already thought of that, Phaedra. He's in the runabout waiting for us."

The elves had finished lashing the statue to the runabout and called to Phaedra and Annika. They hastened to the side of the airship, where the runabout was snugged up tight to the *Northern Queen*. The statue, still wrapped in cloth, sat in the prow. Jan sat in the stern, hands on the controls for the rudder, fins, and air balloon. A massive clockwork raven perched on a bench. It stretched its wings and cawed at them in greeting.

"I am pleased to assist with the gift-bearing mission!" he croaked.

Phaedra smiled. She was fond of the mechanical bird. He helped watch the reindeer herds during the winter, since they grazed far south of the Pole, but Phaedra had felt he might come in handy during their mission, so he'd been temporarily pulled from that duty.

Phaedra and Annika climbed into the runabout and settled onto their bench. The nearly-silent purr of the engine indicated that the magical engine was at work, not the steam-powered one. Phaedra smiled in approval. They wouldn't be invisible, but they could move as quietly as Nick's sleigh.

"Let's take her out, Jan. Head for the Acropolis," Phaedra said.

Jan nodded. The ropes securing the runabout were released, and the runabout drifted from the *Northern Queen*. The purr of the engine grew into a *putt-putt-putt*, and the smaller airship turned and sailed north-east.

Their course was simple to plot since their destination dominated the skyline. Bathed in moonlight, the marble structures on the Acropolis gleamed ghostly-white.

Phaedra sighed another happy sigh. It felt remarkably pleasant to be in her homeland, speaking Greek with people other than Nick. She wondered if they might extend their visit a little longer and have some food. Fresh fish perhaps? The North Pole had begun to modernize, and they had built a wonderfully ornate glass conservatory with a steeply pitched roof, chock-full of edible plants. And while it was wonderful having fresh Kalamata olives, she was still stuck with salt fish and beef during the long winter.

Maybe…maybe she could just stay here awhile? Not return right away to the Pole? The notion was terrifying in its simplicity and attraction.

"Penny for your thoughts, Phaedra?" Annika asked.

"Oh!" Phaedra waved a hand. "I was thinking about staying here for a few extra days…or weeks."

"Stay?" Annika echoed. "Weeks? But there's so much work to be done!"

Phaedra's shoulders sagged. There was a lot, but it wasn't the work, it was the *responsibility*: she supervised harvesting, planting, and food preparation; coordinated household chores; scheduled elf work shifts and reindeer herd migrations; organized weaving and sewing; sorted Nick's mail; and oversaw construction projects—two this year, a new reindeer barn and a high-tech observatory, to better monitor Nick's flight on Christmas Eve. And those were just the tasks associated with support! She assisted with the toy manufacturing and reindeer training as well.

At the North Pole, a bundle of keys, one for each door of the complex, hung from a ring on Phaedra's sturdy belt. Each year, as the gift-bearer operation grew, more elves arrived to assist, more buildings were added, and more keys slid onto the ring on her belt. Her lower back ached most days from the great key-ring dangling from her waist.

What would they do without her?

"You're right, Annika," Phaedra said, managing a brief upturn of her mouth, more of a twitch than a smile. "We have to get started on next year's operation."

And yet, as she watched the Acropolis creep closer, she still wondered, what if—?

Jan slowed the tiny airship as they approached the Acropolis. "Which temple?" he called.

"That one!" Phaedra yelled, pointing. "The Erechtheion, the one with the women!"

The sobbing that had plagued her for so long was much louder now, a keening that made her head ache.

Jan stabilized the runabout and threw ropes over the side. Phaedra grimaced. He wasn't expecting her to shimmy down one of those ropes, was he?

She sighed in relief when Jan climbed down the ropes himself, tying the airship to the temple. As he climbed back up, hand over hand, Phaedra pinned a small brooch to her cloak. The brooch had aethergraph capabilities, and she could use it to talk to Jan.

When Jan was back aboard the runabout, he unrolled a rope ladder. In Phaedra's opinion, the ladder wasn't much better than just sliding down a rope, but she made it to the ground without disaster. Annika dropped down beside her a few minutes later.

Next, Jan lowered the statue. Although it was attached by ropes, it was North Pole magic, which eased the delivery of all manner of gifts all over the world, that kept the airship steady and saw the massive statue safely lowered to the ground.

Together, Annika and Phaedra rolled the wrapped statue to the southern porch of the Erechtheion. Instead of stately, Ionic columns, like those on the northern porch, here five marble women supported the structure with a gaping hole where a sixth should stand. The Caryatids.

Phaedra patted the heavy bundle. "Almost there, lady. I can't believe they locked you up in a museum."

The sobbing abruptly broke off. Hushed words filled her head instead.

"Careful."

"Attend."

"Beware."

"Caution."

"Guard."

Phaedra stared at the five Caryatids. They hadn't moved, but she was certain the whispered warnings had come from them.

"Annika, did you hear that?"

Annika had not wasted time in starting to unwrap the statue. She stopped sawing at a rope with her small knife and looked up. "Rodents, don't you think?"

"Rodents...?" Phaedra held her breath and cocked her head, straining to hear the least sound. Ah, there. A sort of scrabbling, scratching sound. Under ordinary circumstances, she'd be happy to assume mice or rats were the culprits, but she doubted the Caryatids would have warned her about mice.

"Who's there?" she called. She brought her hands together and concentrated. On a gift-bearing night, her North Pole magic was enhanced and she could cast small spells. A ball of light formed between her hands. Parting them, she blew a gentle stream of air at the light. The globe floated away from her, toward the shadows of the temple.

Something cackled. In the silvery light of Phaedra's globe, malformed, black shapes writhed and capered.

"By the Pole, what *are* those things?" Annika gasped.

The creatures shrank from the light, but Phaedra caught glimpses of goats' legs, horns, tusks, spindly tails, and red eyes. She gulped. "I think those are *kallikantzaroi*." At Annika's puzzled shrug, Phaedra added, "Goblins. They only come above ground during the twelve days of Christmas."

Annika resumed hacking at the ropes. "Let's do this quickly then, before they decide to pester us."

Phaedra knelt, pulling her own multi-tool from her pocket.

The Caryatids hissed in her mind, and Phaedra jerked her head up. An inky black thing, the size of a badger, leapt at her. Its mouth gaped open, displaying rows of jagged teeth.

Phaedra pulled her telescoping parasol out of her boot. She raised the metal rod and batted the goblin aside.

Another capering goblin bounded from the shadows.

"Keep at those ropes, Annika!" Phaedra shouted, struggling to her feet. She struck this *kallikantzaros* too as it jumped for her face. It shrieked, smacking into the temple wall and falling to the ground.

Phaedra pressed the brooch pinned to her velvet cloak, activating its aethergraph. "I need Muninn!"

"Yes, Mrs. Claus!" came the crackly response from Jan.

Two *kallikantzaroi* jumped her at once. As she conked one on the head with the parasol rod, the second climbed her shoulders and clawed her face.

She screamed, scrabbling at the goblin.

A raucous caw announced Muninn's arrival. His talons clenched around the goblin and tore it free of Phaedra's shoulders. Muninn strove for altitude. Once he'd risen several feet in the air, he dropped the *kallikantzaros*. It hit the dusty ground with a wet thwap. Muninn cawed, circled, and dove again at the horde of *kallikantzaroi*.

Phaedra staggered, touching her injured cheek. It was wet, and she took away her hand and stared at the blood on her fingers. "What do they want?" she muttered, wiping the blood onto her skirt. The parasol rod slipped in the sweaty grip of her other hand.

"Mischief," echoed in her head.

"Devilment."

"Discord."

"Chaos."

"Pain."

Still more of the goblins emerged from the dark. Phaedra risked a quick glance at Annika. The elf had finished cutting the ropes on one end—sandaled feet peeked out from the loosening oil cloth—and moved to the head, sawing at the ropes there.

A cluster of *kallikantzaroi* gamboled forward, gibbering, long tongues snaking from their mouths. Muninn swooped and dove at them, talons extended. He clutched two, while his mighty wings knocked over the rest.

With cries of *"Danger!"* filling her head, Phaedra tore her eyes away from the mechanical raven. A goblin crouched in front of her, jaw unhinged, fangs glistening. She depressed the button on her parasol rod. It extended another foot, and several smaller spokes popped out from the main rod. Fabric unfurled from the spokes, and within seconds, Phaedra held a beautiful, yet sturdy parasol. She used it as a shield, so that the canopy protected her face and body.

Venom splattered against her parasol. The fabric hissed as the acid burned holes in it.

Before the snake-like goblin could spit at her again, Phaedra pressed the button a second time, collapsing the parasol. She rushed the goblin and hit it on the head with the metal rod. After it keeled over, she stooped, picked it up by one cloven hoof, and hurled it at the Erechtheion.

"Got it!" Annika yelled.

Phaedra spun on her heel and dashed to Annika and the sixth Caryatid. Holding out her hand, she concentrated again. "Come on, need to finish the delivery," she murmured. A weak breeze swirled around her hand. She blew on it, and it flowed from her to the prone statue.

The Caryatid rose from the ground, her oil-cloth covering falling away as she floated to the porch and her five sisters.

Dimly, Phaedra could hear Muninn screeching and cursing as he struggled against the *kallikantzaroi*. But drowning out the sounds of the world around her was a chorus of feminine voices, the five Caryatids rejoicing in the return of their long-lost sister.

The sixth statue slid into her spot, the marble grinding as her head and feet settled into her space, and her voice joined the choir. The sisters' song reached a triumphant crescendo and cut off. As the resonance of the last note rang, a blinding flash of golden light burst from the six Caryatids. Phaedra threw her arms in front of her face, stumbled, and fell to the ground. Shrill screams of pain sounded behind her. Gradually, the light faded, and Phaedra lowered her arms.

The six Caryatids stood in place, dignified women. Important women, as they were holding up a roof with their heads. They weren't human, but they weren't quite stone, either.

"What a heavy load they bear," Phaedra whispered. Tears pricked her eyes.

She stood, wincing as her ankle twinged. Next to her, Annika rubbed her eyes and blinked.

"Is it done?" the elf asked. "Where are those fiends?"

"Gone, I think," Phaedra said. "I heard them screaming. That light probably hurt them."

Annika grunted. "She looks good."

"She does." Phaedra smiled. "Happy, even."

"I'm exhausted," Annika said, yawning. "I can hardly wait to see my bed. Let's go, Phaedra. We'll be back at the North Pole before dawn."

Phaedra hesitated. What harm to stay? To enjoy the sun? No snow, no ice, no lutefisk. It was tempting. She could practically feel the sun warming her face, could taste tangy goat cheese.

"Phaedra?"

Annika stood at the rope ladder, Muninn cradled in her arms. One of the raven's wings hung crookedly, a few talons were missing, and acid burns mottled his body. But his eyes were bright and he cawed.

"I defeated the goblin menace," Muninn croaked.

Chuckling, Phaedra looked again at the Caryatids. The sixth had been pampered and adored in a museum, admired by countless people. Yet, Phaedra had felt her joy at rejoining her sisters, at taking up her share of the burden.

Phaedra squared her shoulders. "Coming, Annika! Do you need me to carry Muninn? He's nearly as big as you!"

As she climbed out of the runabout and onto the deck of the *Northern Queen*, Phaedra knew immediately that something had happened. The elves were bouncing, eyes twinkling and cheeks flushed.

Phaedra sniffed, but didn't detect the odor of spirits. "What's got into everyone?"

The elves all began speaking at once. Phaedra could only decipher snatches of sentences.

"—didn't see anything—"

"—suddenly—"

"—what humans feel—"

"Come look!"

That last was clear enough, and Phaedra allowed herself to be tugged to the captain's room. A large table dominated the cabin; it was the hub of the ship, where meals were shared, meetings held, and courses plotted.

It was covered in food. Platters of cheese and olives, baked fish, dolmathes, and souvlaki. Bowls of tzatziki and salads. Loaves of bread placed at regular intervals along the length of the table. In the center, towering over the other dishes, was a tiered dessert stand, filled with baklava, kourabiedes, loukomi, and nuts. A feast.

Phaedra gawked. "How——?"

"We don't know," said an elf. "It just…appeared. We didn't see anyone, Mrs. Claus!"

"We weren't asleep!" chimed another.

"There's a letter," Annika said, stretching an arm to pluck an envelope that was propped against the tiered dessert plates. She handed it to Phaedra.

My Dear Phaedra,
Kalí chroniá—Happy New Year!
Ágios Vassílis

A gift for her—a taste of her homeland. Tears pricked her eyes again. "Thank you, Ágios Vassílis," she murmured, pressing the letter to her lips.

She slipped the letter into her pocket. "All right, everyone, let's eat!" She caught Annika's gaze and smiled. "No one will notice if we're a little late returning home."

Annika snorted, plucking a small square of loukami from the dessert plates.

Phaedra laughed. Gift-bearing—and the responsibilities that went with it—was good work, hard work, and she was proud to be part of it. But she and Nick needed to talk about periodic pleasure trips. Unlike the Caryatids, she wasn't made of stone.

YOU'D BETTER WATCH OUT
Maren Matthias

The poor mass of black fur scampering across the white field barely had time to blink before the arrow struck its heart. Slinging the crossbow across her back, Fianna strode forward and retrieved her arrow, wiping the blood on the cloth tied around her thigh. "Blasted niddlers, infecting my precious trees."

"Momma!" She turned to find Dover running toward her as fast as his little legs could carry him. He was a scrawny fellow, the smallest and youngest of her adopted children, but what he lacked in size he made up for in persistence and exuberance. "Papa wants you, he says it's urgent."

"Oh, I'm sure it's as urgent as that time he needed to show me his new typewriter or when he needed me to change the light bulb in the bathroom because he forgot where he put the ladder. I have a Christmas tree to chop down."

"Please," Dover pleaded and his big blue eyes made her heart melt.

"Well all right then, but let's make it quick. He better not be messing around in my control room," she muttered to herself as she followed Dover back the way she came. She smiled as the lodge came into view.

In the off-season the "North Pole" was as ever-changing as the whims and fancies of a child, popping around from place to place. Whatever form it took—a Tuscan villa or a house in the jungle (Fianna's personal favorite)—it was always new and exciting. But in December, home always returned to winter and evergreens, the lodge she and Nick had built together—the home they loved most of all. Despite those damn niddlers.

Fianna followed Dover through the back door into her control center where the computers were crunching the naughty and nice numbers—numbers she and Nick would fight about later—and down a series of corridors where jazz music, explosions, and laughter leaked out from behind doorways. She was proud of what they'd constructed. The lodge had been built with a design that looked small and cozy from the outside and took up little space, but was a maze of spacious rooms on the inside with new secrets popping up every now and again to everyone's delight.

Dover led her into the kitchen where Nick beamed at her from behind the island counter.

"Darling!" he crowed. "I think I've finally perfected my sugar cookie recipe! Come, come, have a taste."

"This is the urgent issue you had that couldn't wait until I'd brought back the tree?" she asked sternly, although she couldn't deny how adorable her husband was, giddy and completely covered in flour. She never tired of it.

"He took me away from reindeer training," her eldest, Erin, was sitting on the far edge of the counter, her curved lips peppered with sugar.

"You both always take so long and this couldn't wait. Here."

Fianna accepted the cookie he handed her and took a bite. It *was* perfection. Nick chuckled to himself. She knew he didn't need her opinion to know he'd succeeded; he just wanted to see the look on her face.

"I hate to interrupt..." They all turned to see Damien standing in the doorway. "There's been another abduction. A children's center in Oslo, Norway."

Four sets of eyes zeroed in on Fianna. It was always the same reaction—an eruption of fire followed by a deep breath that wasn't calming enough.

"This calls for Scotch." She'd retrieved four tumblers from the cupboard when Nick came up behind her and wrapped her in his arms.

He knew she would go; it was her self-proclaimed duty. She snuggled against his chest, sighing into the comfort.

"You'll need this," he pulled a small black pouch from his pocket and pressed it into her hand. "Some snow from beneath our favorite tree."

"Ah, thank you, dear one."

"What's so special about snow?" Dover interrupted.

"The tree at the center of the wood was the first tree planted here at the North Pole," Nick explained. "Much like everything else here, the tree is magic, as is the snow that falls around it. We save it for when we need it, but just a sprinkling can do marvelous things."

The sun shone brilliantly on the snow, making it sparkle like diamonds for Fianna's send-off. She had a Thermos of fresh cider from Nick in her deceptively small bag and charms from each of her children pinned to the collar of her cloak. Samuel, their husky, walked beside her on their way to the barn where everyone else was waiting to see her off.

They all tried to look nonchalant, lounging around the barn—except Nick, who was openly pacing—but Fianna could feel the tension and all they succeeded in was looking like constipated statues.

"What a sorry lot you all are. I'll be back in plenty of time for Christmas." Despite the trip she was about to embark on, seeing them all together warmed her down to her toes. Nick kissed the top of her head. "It's the scotch."

"Mmm and love. So much love." She smiled up at him and tugged on his beard, making him chuckle.

After hugs and kisses were exchanged, Fianna moved to a corner of the barn where a small circular dais stood. Azra flipped open the control box on the wall, pressed a couple of buttons, and the dais' surface began to glow. Fianna stepped up and tugged on her tight black gloves. "Give me two days, maybe three," she said.

"I've already opened the betting pool," Erin assured her.

"That's my girl."

Azra flipped a switch and Fianna felt a tingling in her body, starting at her feet. Slowly, she began to disappear, atom by atom, until her family was a blur of color and then all was light. It was a heat rush, transporting this way. When she'd re-materialize it would take a few minutes to get the feeling back in all of her limbs.

She ended up in a narrow, empty street lined with cars and darkened windows. If Azra's coordinates were correct (which they always were), she was a couple blocks from Oslo's center square. She was thankful to be on a deserted street. While nobody would expect a sweet-looking grandma to have a gun hidden beneath her cloak, she didn't want to take any chances. Her boots padded softly on the poorly shoveled sidewalk while she inspected the cars. She stopped and ran a gloved hand along a sleek, white hood. "Yes, you'll do quite nicely I think," she murmured.

Later, while a white Nissan Leaf was speeding along the mountainside, a young man went to his parking spot to find his car missing. In its place was a sturdy box wrapped with a red bow and a letter:

Dear Jim, thank you for lending me the use of your car. I am terribly sorry for the inconvenience, but I assure you it was of the utmost importance and I am eternally grateful. I promise it will be returned within 48 hours in the same condition I found it in. In the box you will find compensation for this loan as well as a dozen of my husband's finest sugar cookies. Merry Christmas, dear Jim. ~ FC.

❄

Anyone else would have marveled at the view out the window but Fianna merely drummed her fingers along the steering wheel and ran through the details in her head. Five abductions in three weeks. She was kicking herself for not taking action after the first disappearance but she hadn't realized they were connected until last week, when the trail had gone cold.

Tucked away just outside of the city, the orphanage was tall and grey, starkly contrasting against its white backdrop. It didn't look terribly cold and unwelcoming, but it didn't seem that comfort and charm was a priority either. She made her way up the stone steps and rapped the shiny doorknocker.

A young, puffy-cheeked face peered out at her curiously. Fianna bent down to eye level and smiled warmly. "Well hello, dear one. Is Mrs. Haugen here?"

"Camilla! What I have told you about answering the door?" a middle-aged woman ran up behind the girl and hugged her around the waist. "Run along now and wash up, it's just about time for lunch." As the girl scampered away the woman stood and considered Fianna with suspicious grey eyes. "Who are you?"

"My name is Fianna O'Connor. I'm here to speak with Mrs. Haugen."

"That's me, what is this regarding?"

"A young girl you have here, Sigrid."

Mrs. Haugen's face paled. "You'd best come with me." She led her through the foyer that was decorated with a warm red rug, the walls covered in paintings by both professional artists and children who'd come through over the years. They entered her office where she had to shoo a couple children away from the windows. They watched Fianna with delight as they crossed to the door. A young boy pulled shyly on her cloak. "Do you have any cookies?" he half-whispered in the way children do.

"Simon, that's very rude!" Mrs. Haugen chided.

"Oh it's quite all right," Fianna assured her. "And in fact I do, but they'd best wait until after lunch hadn't they? Wouldn't want to ruin that appetite of yours, however unlikely that would be." She winked at Simon and was treated to a wide grin in return. Once the children were out and the doors were shut, Mrs. Haugen grabbed a tea tray from the sideboard and set it on the desk between them.

"Please, let me," Fianna insisted. While Mrs. Haugen straightened up the cushions on the window seat Fianna poured the tea, sprinkling a pinch of snow from the pouch at her belt into Mrs. Haugen's cup. People trusted her by nature, but a little bit of magic never hurt. When they sat Fianna could see how tired the matron was in the lines around her eyes and the unsteadiness of her hands.

"What is your interest in Sigrid?"

"I was hoping to speak with you about the possibility of adoption. I realize it's a bit out-of-process to go about it this way, but I was here several months ago with a friend and met Sigrid in the playroom. She showed me her dolls."

"Mrs. O'Connor, I'm afraid I have some bad news. Sigrid was taken away. Kidnapped."

"Oh no, I am so sorry to hear that! How terrible this must be for you. Do they know who took her?"

"I'm afraid not. The police questioned a number of visitors but they all came out clean."

"And nothing on the security cameras?"

"Nothing. The last thing we could see was Sigrid getting up in the middle of the night, I assume to go to the bathroom."

"Hmm. Mrs. Haugen, might I see Sigrid's room?"

"Please know, Mrs. O'Connor," Mrs. Haugen began on their way up the stairs, "that I would never neglect these children. I'm not able to have any so I feel as if they were my own."

"I understand that completely. Don't blame yourself. There are monsters out there that even we mothers overlook."

"Here is Sigrid's room. She shares it with a few others." The room had two bunk beds with chests at each end. "That's hers." She pointed to the bottom bunk closest to the window. The bed looked as if it had never been slept in, stuffed animals cuddled up by the pillow, a few games set out neatly by the foot. Fianna picked up a small green handheld video game. "This wasn't Sigrid's."

"No, it belonged to a volunteer who moved out of the country a few months back. Sigrid liked the game so much he left it for her."

"Might I take it with me?" Fianna smiled and added a twinkle to her eye.

Mrs. Haugen blinked. "Of course."

"Thank you for your time, Mrs. Haugen. You've been most helpful."

"Of course, Mrs. O'Connor. Let me know if you need anything else."

On her way back to the car Fianna pressed the jewel on her ring and adjusted the back of her earring until the static calmed. After two rings Nick answered.

"Sweetheart! How's it going?"

"So far so good. Are you with Damien? I need you guys to locate Tristan Wilder for me. What's that sound?"

"Dover and Erin are testing the paintball guns. Tristan Wilder? You mean that kid who completely took apart and rebuilt everything we gave him?"

"That's the one."

"Smart kid. I always liked him."

"I think he's the guy I'm looking for."

"Ah. It's always a damn shame to see a good nut go bad. Give me a moment, I'll grab Damien."

Fianna leaned against the hood of the car and contented herself with listening to her children play in the background while admiring the cliffs in the distance. She adored Norway. She'd have to bring Dover to see the fjords; he would love them.

"He's in France." Nick's voice sounded in her ear. "In a small house just outside of Rouen. We're sending the coordinates now."

Her thin steel bracelet flashed and location coordinates engraved themselves into the silver. "Got them. Give Damien my thanks." Pressing the jewel on her ring again, she ended the call.

She pulled out the black pouch and sprinkled some snow on the car's hood ornament. "Time to send you home." She watched as the car flickered and disappeared, and then shook a handful of snow into her palm. It was a shame to waste the snow, but she didn't have the time or patience to deal with airports. "France, here we come," she said, and threw the snow over her. Traveling by snow was as exhilarating as the teleport pad was disorienting. Enveloped in cold and white, she felt as if she was flying with the clouds, a feeling she never tired of.

She landed in a bounce on her feet in a deserted alley. The unfortunate thing about snow travel is that while it felt like no time at all, it was actually the slowest form of magical transportation. It was only lunchtime when she left Norway and here it was already dark. Thankfully she'd been to Rouen recently and knew exactly which hotel to stay at. As she navigated the lamp lit streets from memory, she made another call.

While the morning sun shone through the windows Fianna pulled her long hair into an elegant twist. Unicorn hair, Nick liked to call it. Diamond earrings that sang old money graced her ears and a fitted black pantsuit of the latest French style completed the look nicely. It was a good thing she kept a fitness room in the house—complete with aerial silks and a boxing ring—or she didn't know if she'd have fit into the suit with all of the baking Nick did. She observed her handiwork in the mirror. She looked damn good for being hundreds of years old, if she did say so herself.

Pierre greeted her outside of the hotel with a warm hug and a kiss on each cheek.

"Thank you for doing this, Pierre."

"I should be thanking you, we've been after this guy for awhile. He's a slippery one, though, right when we thought we had him he'd disappear. You're an angel, Momma C." He gestured to the car they'd be using. "I got a chauffeur's hat for the occasion."

Fianna grimaced. She didn't like being in the backseat of a car. She felt too vulnerable. But if this was going to work she needed to convince anyone watching that she was a wealthy woman who was too important to drive herself places. She never understood why that always impressed people. Lazy and entitled, she called it.

"Always the showman, and now a detective. What a fine young man you've become."

"Is that all you have?" He gestured to the small black clutch in her hand.

She winked. "Oh it's made with a bit of Christmas magic. We'd best be off. But before we go you need to promise me that you'll remain safe. If you hear gunshots you drive off as fast as you can. Understood?"

Pierre laughed. "This isn't my first rodeo, Momma C. And I couldn't just leave you stranded."

"Don't worry about me, I have my own ways of getting around— just promise me you'll stay safe."

"I promise."

She kissed him on the cheek. "Good boy. Now let's go save those kids."

They pulled up in front of a modest house that looked as if it had been built in the 18th century, at least ten miles from its nearest neighbor. As they parked in the circular drive a scrawny, scruffy fellow scurried down the front steps to greet them.

"Madame Lucelle."

"Mr. Wilder."

"Please come in. Your driver will stay outside, yes? I must say, your timing is excellent. When I received your call I was delighted to have a woman of such fine standing be our first client of the season. You beat the Christmas rush! Although it wasn't very clear on the phone what you're looking for. We have clients looking for servants, test subjects—" He grinned with eyebrows raised. "—companions." Fianna fought a wave of nausea.

"A house girl I can keep under my complete control. Maids are getting more expensive and rather frivolous with their favors."

"I'm sure we'll have just what you're looking for, Madame. We usually prepare a couple of our best options for the clientele to sample and peruse, but you seemed adamant about taking a look at the whole lot at once." He hesitated, as if hoping she would change her mind.

"That's right."

Nodding and breathing audibly, he unlocked a door and led her down a flight of stairs into a cellar. She'd seen plenty of horror stories over the years, but they never ceased to hurt her heart and make her stomach churn. They were all there, the five recent kidnappings and dozens more. They were chained to the concrete floor, huddled together for warmth. They were dirty, malnourished, and none of them would meet her eye. She longed to comfort them, but she had to play Madame Lucelle for a bit longer.

"Well, it looks like you've been in business for quite some time, Mr. Wilder."

"Indeed, Madame." The pride in his voice was sickening.

Sweet, young Tristan. What happened to you? She knelt in front of a small girl with long blonde hair and cold feet. Her finger lifted Sigrid's chin and as her own green eyes gazed into blue-flecked grey, she felt the girl's heart skip a beat, and a seed of warmth began to bloom in her chest. Fianna kept her gaze composed. *I'm going to get you out of here.* "This one, I think. Yes, she will do nicely."

"An excellent choice, Madame. I picked that one up just the other day."

"Shall we go upstairs and discuss the details?"

"This way to my office." He seemed less sure than the boy she once knew him to be. He was flustered, nervous, with insecurity embedded deep within that she didn't recognize.

Once they were shut up in his office she looked him square in the eye. "Tristan. When did you become like this? You used to be such a lovely boy."

He stopped and stared. "I'm sorry...what?"

"You always were intelligent, and you could have done so much good. That's one reason you were given this for your eighth Christmas." Pulling the game out of her clutch behind her back— seemingly out of nowhere—she threw it on the desk.

He scrambled to grab his gun from the drawer and aimed it for her chest, but his hands couldn't keep it steady. "Who are you?"

"I'm their mother. I know every one of their names. I know their biggest dreams and their greatest fears. And I used to know yours. I'm the one who made sure you got that handheld. And I'm the one who's going to make sure these children get home." In the blink of an eye she'd pulled the gun from her clutch and shot him in the foot. Ignoring his screams, she picked up the gun he dropped and turned to face the burly men bursting through the door.

"Gentlemen," she greeted cordially. She allowed one to disarm her and pull her into a backward chokehold. She preferred scrappy fighting anyway. Using the leverage of the arm around her throat she slashed the other in the jugular with her heel before flipping the first over her back and onto his head. "Well. That was anticlimactic." Just then a third darkened the doorway and a gunshot rang out. He fell dead in front of her, revealing Erin with a shotgun poised, Azra coming up behind her.

"Hey mom!" they grinned.

"What are you girls doing here?"

"Oh, you know. Things were getting boring at home, thought we'd help out." Erin nudged one of the unconscious men with her foot. "Nice work."

A tomahawk flew out of Azra's hand past their heads. It caught Tristan in the chest and the machete he'd raised clattered to the floor beside his limp form.

"Yea," Azra continued, "The boys are testing everything they make and it's annoying as hell. Needed to get away for a day or two."

"Well I'm glad you're here." She turned to the man at her feet. "Such a tragic end for a promising lad." Erin wrapped her arm around Fianna's shoulders.

"You can't raise everyone, momma."

"I know. Come along, let's get those kids back home. Leave those weapons up here, why don't you, the poor things are scared half to death. And take this." She tossed them the pouch of snow. "Use it on the shackles." While Erin and Azra disappeared into the cellar, Pierre came running up to the house. "Didn't I tell you to drive away as fast as you can?"

He grinned. "Now what kind of detective would I be if I ran from the scene of the crime? I called backup. They should be here shortly so you might want to make this quick."

"We'll be gone and you can tell of your heroic deed." She gestured to the office. "They're in there. Four of them."

Pierre pulled her in for a hug. "Thank you, Momma C."

"Thank you, Pierre."

"Momma," Erin came over. "We have most of them safe and cozy in the van, but one of them insists she waits for you."

"Van? What van?"

Azra grinned. "I might have added a few perk buttons to the sleigh's dash."

"Of course you did." Fianna laughed heartily. "What would I do without you all? Sprinkle the children with snow, would you? They'll believe this all to be a dream, which will decrease their trauma, and I'll go get Sigrid."

Sigrid sat where Fianna left her, still as stone. Fianna settled cross-legged in front of the girl and spoke softly. "My name is Fianna Claus. You're Sigrid, aren't you?"

The girl nodded. "Are you magic?"

Fianna chuckled. "What makes you ask that?"

"You feel like magic. And the nice girls broke our shackles with snow."

"Yes, that is magic snow. It's from my home, the North Pole."

Sigrid said nothing.

"You know, Mrs. Haugen is very worried about you," Fianna continued and Sigrid nodded. "Those girls are my daughters, Erin and Azra. I also have two sons, Damien and Dover, and my husband, Nick. I think you might like them very much. I know they'd like you. I wonder, Sigrid, would you like to come home with us? I can be your mother."

Sigrid was silent and Fianna waited patiently. Then Sigrid crawled forward and curled herself into Fianna's lap. Fianna ran her fingers through her hair and kissed the top of her head. "Come, it's time to go home."

❄

"Does everybody have what they need? Popcorn? Blankets? Whiskey? It's going to be a long night, let's get settled in."

They'd outfitted a corner of her control room with a sectional and a flat-screen so the family could all watch Christmas together. Sigrid was nestled in Erin's lap as her new sister braided ivy into her hair. Azra held the popcorn bowl with Samuel settled at her feet while Damien sat at the computer to Fianna's right, headphones waiting around his neck. Dover had insisted on going with Papa on his rounds, and not even Momma C. could resist his endearing blue eyes.

"All right," she said, turning on her headset. "Papa C. do you read me?"

"Aye, my darling, I read you."

"Grand. We're picking up movement at the Watson's. Seems little Angie wants to catch a glimpse of Santa."

"Roger that."

Fianna looked over at her family celebrating the greatest tradition they'd ever have together, and felt her eyes start to well.

"It's the scotch." Damien squeezed her hand.

"And love." She squeezed back. "So much love."

CAPTAIN LIZZY AND THE STRANGER IN THE FOG

Anne Luebke

Lizzy stared at the fog and sighed. At least the upper deck was quiet—all the passengers were staying down in the dining area. Lizzy had even authorized the bar to stay open past the normal closing time. This was going to be a long night, but they should still make landing tonight even if the fog didn't let up.

She had some regrets about attempting the New York to Chicago route, especially the timing, but staying in New York over Christmas wasn't something she was prepared to do. If she'd stayed she would have been expected to visit her nephew and his new husband for the holidays. Which would be weird. Their home was just a bit too, well, homey. Two kids running around and fresh-baked cookies in those fancy bowls that can only be used once a year. And Lizzy had already sent the gifts. It would be odd to send gifts and then show up at their door. What if they had opened them early? It would be so awkward.

So no staying in New York. Instead, she had advertised the New York to Chicago route—"Be Home for the Holidays!" And they would have made it in plenty of time if it hadn't been for the darn fog. Even with her fancy new airship there wasn't much to be done.

The ZC-710 was the latest and greatest, with all the new safety features and a proprietary helium to hydrogen mixture, but it couldn't do a darn thing about the fog. Turning on the safety lights (in case of pirate attack) only made it worse. The lights reflected back in the fog and Lizzy had ordered that whoever had the bright idea of turning them on should be sent below in a basket until they could give the exact altitude of the ship over the lake. She was only half joking.

For the last three hours all her requested updates from the tower had come back with various types of soup in the little column where the weather report belonged. Any other day and that sort of behavior would be reportable, but Lizzy figured they only had some poor intern working on the holiday and there's no reason to spoil what little fun the kid had. The only issue had been when her navigator started worrying about hail when the tower had come back with Matzo Ball as the latest variety of soup. Lizzy patiently explained the origins of the joke while her navigator ranted.

At least she didn't have to worry about running into anything. On a clear night there might have been some parties taking a spin around the city but the fog would have grounded those plans. No point in raising a toast to the city skyline when you can't even see the hand in front of your face. The tower had only warned her of one other ship, a cargo zep headed south, and Lizzy hadn't bothered to get the name. She'd have to be pretty darn far off course before she ran into them and the ZC's nav was second to none. Even going two days without a decent bearing hadn't affected their course.

They were making progress. She could hear the hum of the engines, feel the heat expelled by the steam that coursed through the metal of the ship like its lifeblood. But without any reference points, not even a faint glow where the tower should be, it felt like they were standing still.

And then there was a light, a faint red glow moving faster than her ship and overtaking it. Not pirates, the engine of the approaching zep was too quiet for that. Even in the fog you'd hear a pirate ship coming long before it got close. Sure, they'd be sitting ducks in the fog if she was wrong, but Lizzy was never wrong. That's why she was the captain.

"Ahoy there," called out a voice from the general direction of the red light.

"Ahoy yourself," answered Lizzy.

"What are you doing out on such a foggy night?" asked the stranger. Lizzy still couldn't get a good look at him or his ship.

"I could ask you the same thing." Lizzy was getting testy. She didn't like talking to the fog. She had a perfectly workable radio for this sort of thing. Of course, he probably didn't. Probably a hobbyist flying some home grown airship without the proper permits.

He laughed. "Fair question. Are you Captain Elizabeth Holden of the passenger ship *Bethany*?"

Lizzy nodded and then realized he couldn't see in the fog either. "Yes, I am. Although I don't know why you'd want to come out here to find me. We're docking in Chicago soon."

Another laugh from the fog. "Sure you are. But you've got two little passengers who will be wanting their Christmas presents and now is as good a time as any. Catch!"

An oddly shaped object flew out of the fog and Lizzy dove to catch it before the delicate paper hit the dampness of the wooden deck. "What's this?" she asked. The tag said it was for Melody Erpenbach. Melody was a seven year old girl, daughter of James T. Erpenbach, the railroad tycoon and the reason that Lizzy had to upgrade and spend most of her life savings for a new zep.

James T. Erpenbach had used the war to his advantage. While all the zeps were off fighting, he had built his empire on dependability— "Ship with Erpenbach and get it there intact!"

Well, little Melody is certainly rich enough for her father to send gifts by airmail. Lizzy looked at the little package. "What is it?" she asked while squishing it cautiously.

"A stuffed giraffe," came the voice. That explained the shape of the package. Melody had recently gotten back from safari with her mother. They were head back to Chicago to spend Christmas with her father.

Lizzy shook her head and then kicked the ship when she figured out the stranger still couldn't see her. "I don't think she'll like it much," said Lizzy.

"Why not?" At least the stranger seemed interested and not dismissive.

"She didn't like the safari. She said her mother kept trying to toughen her up but she hated the guns and the blood and the dead animals."

"I suppose that wouldn't be much fun for a little girl," chuckled the stranger.

"Not this particular little girl at any rate," replied Lizzy. She hated when people made assumptions based on gender. After all it's not like Lizzy herself had ever conformed to gender norms. Wearing a skirt on a zep was sure to get you caught in the rigging and any 'girlyness' could be interpreted as a sign of weakness by the crew. Weakness could mean the crew wouldn't follow directions in an emergency and that could get everyone killed.

"What do you think she would like? A dolly that talks?"

Lizzy shook her head and then mentally kicked herself again. Stupid fog. "No, what she'd like is a train set. I know that's not the typical present for a girl her age but she's been missing her dad. I'm sure he would love to help her set it up."

Lizzy heard some rustling then another package hurtled out of the fog. It did rattle like a train set under the bright colored paper. How much stuff did this guy have with him?

"Now what should little Billy get for Christmas?" asked the delivery guy.

Billy was Melody's little brother. He'd been hanging around with Lizzy most of the afternoon, but hadn't talked much. "Some building blocks. So he can help his father and sister with the train set. And I think he'd like this giraffe quite a bit more than Melody."

Another package out of the fog, and Lizzy was ready this time. She had the other packages on the deck in a safe spot before she reached out to catch it. "How is it that you are so sure of what the children want?" asked the voice in the fog.

"I listen. Talking with the passengers and building up trust is how a good airship captain stays in business. There's hundreds of other ships out there but my passengers seek me out because they know me. They know that I'll take care of them and get them to their destination safely and comfortably. The actual sailing of the ship is something any old pilot can do but building up a good reputation is what makes a great captain." She had memorized this speech ages ago but seldom had a chance to use it. One day she should write a memoir or something. Although they'd probably want her to spend most of the book on pirate battles. Not that it was a minor thing or something, but it wasn't what Lizzy liked to talk about.

"You know, you sound like a wise woman. I'd love to get to know you better." The pickup line sounded out of place in the middle of the air over Lake Michigan. Not that Lizzy got many of them. She was too ambitious to spend time dating. If she was meeting a man it was for a business contact, not for romance. Dating the crew was something she'd never permit herself to do. The captain should be above all that, more feared than loved. Respect from her crew was worth more than anything romantic.

"You want to meet in person sometime?" she asked doubtfully. It seemed unlikely that they'd ever see each other again. Not that they were exactly seeing each other now. Could he even see her?

"This is my busy season. What about April first on top of the Empire State Building?"

Lizzy caught herself before the nod. "Sure, why not?" Then she realized the joke. "Oh, right, April Fool's Day."

"We can make it the second if it helps you feel better." Lizzy was almost reassured. Almost.

"April first is fine. At least it is easy to remember. I'll wear a blue dress."

"And I'll wear a jingle bell. Have a Merry Christmas!"

Lizzy watched the faint red light move away in the fog until she decided it was only the reflection of the lights of her zep and not that of the delivery guy.

April first came quickly. The blue dress, the only one she owned, barely fit. The gold corset she tried to wear over it did not fit. Stupid corset. She took it off for the third time and loosened the laces again. Any looser and she'd have to give up on it. Not like it mattered. Once this guy got a good look at her he'd run off. If he had ever been serious about this to start with.

Corset finally on, she grabbed her coat and swung down the rope to the top of the building. The ESB was lit up in pink tonight. She greeted the staff and picked up a cocktail. At least this location was good. Only other pilots could enter the lounge. She stared at each of the men in turn until she finally spotted the little jingle bell on the lapel of the man's coat. Well, he wasn't bad looking. The beard looked better on him than on most men. Not that she liked beards much. But being picky is what got her here in the first place.

"Hey, you came." Not the best greeting, but not the worst.

"I didn't see you there. I was looking for a blue dress." Oh darn. She looked down, yep, red coat was the only thing showing.

"Sorry, it was cold out." Then she caught sight of yet another gift. "Is that for another over-privileged child?"

"No, it is for you." He handed the gift over. He looked nervous. He really shouldn't be. Not at his age.

She tore off the fancy paper and stared at the doll underneath. It was the kind that shut her eyes when laid to bed. Lizzy had asked Santa for it when she was six and she had been so disappointed when she didn't get it. She didn't remember how long ago it had been before she had forgotten about the doll. It had been a long time.

Long before her hair went white. Before she figured out that her 'experienced' crewmates were half her age. Heck it was probably even back when corsets fit her properly.

Sometimes Lizzy wished she were more sentimental or that she had more space in her tiny apartment. For years any gift that wasn't immediately useful had been regifted as soon as she could think of the proper recipient. Maybe one of her many young grandnieces would appreciate an old fashioned doll. Lizzy certainly couldn't think of a use for it. Now a warm muff, that would have been nice.

She sighed and took the arm of her blind date. "We need to work on your gift giving."

AGATHA SINGS TO THE SCORPIONS
Jeff Kuykendall

Agatha Stewart tightened the red helmet into the ring about her neck and twisted it until the green glow at the lower edge of her vision clicked on. Her breath blasted against the polycarbonate visor, fogging her vision before the cooling system cycled the humidity away. The armed guard let her into the dark airlock, its two doors hissing apart like thick white teeth. Within the small chamber, rows of lights in the walls blinked on, though just flickered and flickered.

The strobing gave her a headache. Everything was off today. The suit felt too large. Her ankles chafed in the oversized, heavily weighted boots. Frank wasn't here.

Two security officers wheeled her large crate in behind her. Fifteen minutes had passed since she'd seen the container last, as Pantheon Security—in this case, a smiling young woman with a badge that said Callie K.—ran a complete check on it. The crate was sealed by magnetic locks and stamped with *PCR* above the insignia of a reindeer silhouette and the words *Pantheon Crisis Relief.* A green belt of jingle bells was hitched to the coupler and draped over the lid like a tablecloth, and it rang cheerfully as the crate shook, a sound that seemed dislocated from the pressurized corridor and coldly gleaming spacesuits.

"I'll be accompanying you," Callie K.'s voice crackled over the intercom in Agatha's helmet. Agatha took a closer look at her. She appreciated Callie's wide, irresistible smile, because the thick suits didn't allow for much in the way of personality. On the officer's arm was a patch representing the Saragossa Terra colony here on Iapetus: ringed Saturn, spheres for its moons, and the silver eagle of Pantheon swooping in with its talons.

Callie added, "Officer Tulip is coming along too."

Tulip loomed over her, a colossus to defy his name. On his back was a black laser rifle, and at his hip was a pistol, which he indicated to Agatha with a gentle pat. "Scorpions move fast," he said. "Don't worry, I'm a quick draw."

Agatha didn't see the humor. "They're children," she said.

"Children with stingers."

The airlock doors closed their jaws behind them. Agatha had a flash of an identical airlock two weeks ago. Frank Stewart wasn't making eye contact with anyone, but was annoying the hell out of the security guard by leaning against the crate beside her and softly singing "Santa Baby" in his best Eartha Kitt while Agatha tried not to laugh. Half an hour later, during the gift-giving, the blast lit the vacuum where they stood, a brief burst like a flashbulb; she was on the opposite end of the great hold but Frank was right on top of—

"Where's Santa?" said Officer Tulip.

The room was rumbling. It wasn't just an airlock; it was an elevator, descending by several levels.

Callie K. punched his arm and gave him a shut-up look. "You were on Io?" Tulip asked. "And your Santa—?"

"My husband," said Agatha, not looking at him.

"They're always couples," Callie said to Tulip. "Mr. and Mrs. Claus. Or Mr. and Mr. Claus."

"Or Mrs. and Mrs.," said Agatha. "Two years ago it was Julia and Jolene Hasselback." The elections came in four year cycles, and Frank and Agatha had been voted in by a healthy majority. After Frank's death, Agatha was given the option to take a leave of absence or step down, but she wouldn't do either.

"I apologize," said Officer Tulip. "I didn't know. Snowfall took credit for that attack."

"Yes," said Agatha, "The terrorists are targeting children now."

It was lucky that none of the young refugees were killed, though a dozen were injured. The casualties were limited to two Pantheon security officers and Frank.

"Scorpions," corrected Tulip.

The rumbling stopped and the doors opened. Oxygen hissed free, and she felt it rippling around her spacesuit. Before them sprawled one shadow-draped stretch of the Engelier basin, the gliding surface composed of grayish ice, the moon's dominant feature. The encampment was bordered by pillars that looked like barrels stacked on top of one another. One section of the colony station formed a ceiling above, blocking any view of space and preventing the refugees from floating upward. Many of them were on the ceiling, clustered together like sea anemone. Others were pressed against the fence, whose narrow gaps between the pillars were just small enough to prevent the young Scorpions from escaping.

Tulip's voice snapped across the feed: "Lights please."

Rectangular bands of light burst from within shallow recesses of the ceiling. A small collection of Scorpions dropped loose and drifted downward, resembling a school of coiled seahorses. Each was about two feet across when balled up, but they could stretch much longer with their stingers out.

As Agatha took a step forward with her weighted red boots, one Scorpion rolled toward her, bumped up against her toe, and looked up with black eyes, a face like white ceramic, and a grin much broader than a human's. Yet it was most certainly a smile, and a friendly one. Most colonists were unnerved by the humanoid qualities of the Scorpions. The face matched neither the serpentine body nor the six stubby little legs. In full grown Scorpions those legs could lift them twice as tall as a human, or telescope in collapse and retract within their carapace. The spiral of a tail, with its down-turned stinger, could also grow, adding to that caricature of a monster that circulated in extreme right-wing circles. "Scorpion" was just the colonists' appellation, but it had stuck like a brand.

This wasn't a monster. The child was beaming. He—and it was a he, she could tell by the yellow stripes zig-zagging across his rust-colored body—had recognized the red of her suit and the crate with the jingle bells.

Of course those jingle bells couldn't jingle outside, but they had symbolic value. Christmas had come to Iapetus. Mrs. Claus was here. She lifted the child into her arms and carried him as she walked deeper into the refugee camp.

Only one adult Scorpion was here, a nurse who had automatically camouflaged against the pillars when the lights switched on, a talent and an instinct belonging only to adults. Now color rippled across a six-legged body shaped like a spiral seashell, her tail drifting loosely behind and above her, and in the fractional gravity she approached with grace. Agatha detected Tulip removing his rifle.

Adult Scorpions had the capacity to communicate with humans, but only in the sign language which humans had taught them. She signed now using two of her pinkish five-pronged claws: *Hello, Mom C-L-A-U-S*. *Mom* Claus, not *Mrs.*, which she could have spelled M-R-S if she wanted to sign it.

Agatha moved toward the nurse, signing back, *Happy Christmas*; Christmas was a wreath-like shape.

The nurse made the military salute which indicated faith in Pantheon, and Agatha smiled politely, but did not return it. She was not an officer that needed to be saluted.

She stepped into the center of the camp with Callie K. pushing the crate behind her. A large screen in the ceiling lit up, and a video played of Mr. and Mrs. Claus—the traditional, portly, Coca-Cola variety—silently dancing amidst elves in a North Pole workshop. Colonial propaganda perhaps, but because of films like these she was welcomed here, a figure of Earthling mythology that the young Scorpions embraced. Earth was about Christmas. Earth, and its Pantheon of colonies, was about toys. As she walked toward the center, her strides exaggerated by the miniscule gravity even in her weighted boots, the small Scorpions showered from the alcoves above, toppled from the pillars, and rolled along the icy surface.

She wanted Frank here, but she tried not to think of him. His mumbled singing of "Santa Baby," his red beard disguised by a false white one, his smile almost as wide as the children's—she willed herself to forget, but then came the memory of the bright brief burst of the explosion, a spark of a scream in the speakers by her ears, the debris shooting outward in straight lines, shrapnel ripping the arm of her suit so that she had to switch to emergency life support.

CRUSH ALL SCORPIONS, Snowfall transmitted in their strange smoldering text, words that broke into broadcasts across all the colonies. SNOW FALLS ON EVERYTHING.

No sympathy for the children. A little Scorpion will grow into a big Scorpion. In the Kuiper Belt, soldiers had reported what they called "Bull Scorpions" the size of shuttlecraft. Yet among the Scorpions there existed a sizable faction of Pantheon sympathizers, refugees who wanted nothing to do with the decades-long conflict. These were undergoing indoctrination in the ways of colonial culture. The camps were a part of this, as was the separation from their children. In some ways, Agatha thought, the ignorance of these young Scorpions was a good thing. They didn't know that before they would age out of the camp their stingers would be surgically removed.

Snowfall had come into existence four years ago, at first affiliated with the more extreme right-wing broadcasts and message boards that objected to the integration of Scorpion refugees into Pantheon. Agatha had never properly understood their complaints. No Scorpion had been incorporated into society. And although Scorpions could survive in an environment or atmosphere with oxygen, none had even left the camps. Each Pantheon colony had its own elected governor, granted enough autonomy that they could refuse any resettlements in their territory. And this stance had been taken from one end of the solar system to the other, the governors caving to pressure from their more vocal constituents. The Scorpions stayed in their cages.

Now fully surrounded by the children, which crawled harmlessly over one another and even leapt in great bounces, alarming Officer Tulip, Agatha unsealed the locks and lifted the lid. The presents looked like the presents they would have watched on the great screen above them. Red and green wrapping paper, golden ribbons with bows on the top. She distributed the packages one at a time, and as each Scorpion received it, the little claws tore through the wrapping paper, opened the box, revealed a toy donated to the PCR by the colonies.

Action figures, matchbox cars, dolls, storybooks, crayons and coloring books; it didn't matter that they were manufactured for oxygen-breathing humans (once, someone had donated a squirt gun). The Scorpions loved them because they had seen all the latest toy commercials, broadcast alongside old Santa movies in the months leading up to Christmas. They knew more about the cartoon pushing the latest line of miniature ponies than they did the geology of their homeworld, which they had never seen. Hell, they knew what ponies were. Ponies were little horses with rainbows on their hindquarters. Cars drove along highways on a distant planet called Earth, and the Scorpions presumed that for the cars to transform into robots was an everyday thing.

"Watch it, watch it," Tulip kept warning Agatha and Callie. "Watch that tail, it almost grazed you." His rifle occasionally lifted but never quite aimed.

Callie finally laughed at him. "Lighten up. It's Christmas."

"I'll lighten up when it's not Christmas."

One by one, the gifts disappeared. Wrapping paper and ribbons like streamers drifted in a weightless cloud around them. Agatha started to sing "Santa Baby." She couldn't help it. Frank was with her somehow, or she was willing him here, like an incantation.

Then her fingers grazed something which didn't match the uniformity of the gift packages: an errant ridge, something hard and metallic. A clumsy little Scorpion briefly covered her visor, and she pushed him gently aside, sending droplets of his chrome-colored urine to trace his slow, somersaulting retreat.

Buried beneath the last of the presents was what looked like an absurdly large horse pill. A protruding band marked one end where it might unscrew apart. She reached for it, but a gloved hand seized her wrist.

Callie still wore her beautiful smile. Her voice came crackling through: "Snow falls on everything."

"Get back, get back!" Agatha called, but she knew that the Scorpions couldn't hear. She waved her arms to scatter them and quickly signed to the nurse, *Run*.

Tulip said, "What's the—"

At his back, from within his center life support, came an electric flare. Torn fabric fluttered from all sides. Something had been planted on him, was triggered. He groped at nothing, his rifle slipping free of his fingers.

Callie K. took it from him and fired once at his chest, a straight blue beam that passed right through him. He fell over slowly, the low gravity reluctantly permitting his weight to topple. Then Callie turned the nozzle on Agatha.

"Shame about your husband," she said.

Knowing others were listening, Agatha said, "This is Agatha Stewart reporting a terrorist attack in the Scorpion holding facility."

Callie hesitated, glancing down at the crate of presents and the white pill-shaped explosive within. Then she checked her watch, part of her gear and strapped to the wrist of her sleeve. "Oh," she said.

"Forty-five more seconds."

"It's the Pantheon security officer named Callie," Agatha said, trying to keep her breathing to a steady pace while her arms continued to shift the Scorpions away.

They had taken notice of the attack on Officer Tulip. Their wide, black eyes watched as his body awkwardly folded onto the gray ice. A dozen were bounding toward the nurse, who scooped them up into her spindly limbs while making a gesture of warning that only they could properly understand. The mask-like quality of her Scorpion features had wrinkled in rippling elliptical shapes, as if her whole face were furrowing with anger.

Callie said to Agatha, "You can run now."

Agatha laughed in disbelief.

"You can be the witness," Callie said. "I only need the Scorpions." But then she squeezed the trigger, and Agatha thought she'd changed her mind that quickly.

The blue beam crossed six inches above her right shoulder.

It connected with the nurse's carapace. The limbs unfolded in shock, and she dropped three of the children. The ripples in her face softened and smoothed, and the black eyes closed as she drifted backward. Six tiny fragments of shell floated sluggishly free.

Agatha screamed into her mic. She hunched and felt her whole body wrenching in shock.

"Twenty seconds," said Callie. "Seventeen. Sixteen."

At the airlock door far behind the woman, twin lamps lit red, a sign that the elevator was descending. Pantheon security was on its way, but they wouldn't arrive in time.

Agatha shut her eyes but still saw, scorched there, the floating shards of the nurse's broken carapace. "Thirteen," said Callie. "Twelve."

And Agatha launched her body at Callie's. In the low gravity she drew an arc above the Snowfall agent, and she reached down and grabbed the nozzle of the rifle with both hands and tried to jerk it free. Callie held tight and pulled the trigger. The blue line sliced straight through both of Agatha's palms and further, through her shoulder blade and out her back. It was like a Scorpion's sting—just a little one, but she couldn't close her hands. Her body kept moving through space. She twisted and saw thousands of beads of blood escaping her suit while the speakers honked in warning at her and the life support struggled to engage, the oxygen hissing out of her chest and her back and through her gloves, drawing air from down her sleeves, like someone trying to suck her through a straw.

She twisted around again, uncontrollable, and saw something strange: Callie with a young Scorpion completely covering her face. The visor was broken, triangular pieces of clear polycarbonate descending about her like a sinking broken crown, and the yellow stripes of the Scorpion were searing white, its tail fully extended and puncturing the throat of Callie K.

Yet, for a moment, a sound came through the speakers, and it belonged not to Callie but to the male Scorpion with the glowing golden bands. Amidst the hissing of air it trilled fiercely. Callie's gloves let go of the stolen rifle. Agatha belatedly hit the ground, and she rolled and bled.

As the timer ran down, the nearest Scorpions fell upon her fast. They blanketed her from head to boots in the instant before the explosive flashed. She felt their bodies stiffen at the blast's surge, and as a unit they rocketed away and smashed against the wall nearest the airlock doors.

She felt both smothered to suffocation and miraculously sustained. The holes in her spacesuit and her gloves were sealed, at least until the Scorpions moved. The life support system chugged on, and stale air began to circulate in the helmet. But her body and her hands ached badly where she had been shot.

She opened her eyes and saw that the Scorpions on her round visor were shifting and tightening. The males were glowing golden, the females a dimmer orange in speckles along their bellies, and the tails and stingers twitched and intertwined and held one another like a hundred hands. She gasped with relief. They were uninjured by the blast. But of course they were! They were denizens of deep space, and there was so little known about them even after all these years of conflict.

Through a gap, Agatha could see a slice of the monitor in the ceiling still playing an old Christmas musical. Santa and Mrs. Claus were feeding the reindeer in joyful silence, their lips moving, the elves around them dancing to nothing at all. How could it mean anything to the little Scorpions if they had never heard music? It was a fat man in a suit, and the beard wasn't even convincing. Mrs. Claus had a warm cherubic face and white hair in a bun. She did a jig while Santa clapped, and the elves, well, they were just children in tacky costumes.

She could hear something soft coming from the Scorpions. The sounds seemed to vibrate through her body. They were trilling, they were humming, they were too young to learn sign language, but they were a music of emotion. A single impulse, a communication that shook her suit and sent the stale air fluttering. *Mother. Mother, please be safe.*

Agatha started to sing "Santa Baby," while the speakers of her intercom crackled with unintelligible human voices calling for her, broken syllables, sharp bursts of noise. She could think of nothing else but "Santa Baby." She sang, snug in the Scorpion pile, her back pinned against the icy surface of the moon, her best Eartha Kitt, and the Scorpions listened.

RED TO HIDE THE BLOOD
Hayley Stone

Alaska, 1964

By the time Nick sent for me, it was already too late.

The lead deer were gone. Not a trace remained beyond their fancy leather harnesses, chewed damn near to pieces, and frosted over with saliva. As for the survivors, I doubted they'd ever have the nerve to fly again. Blitzen almost strangled himself when I held a hand out to his nose, and it took several elves to calm him long enough for me to cut him free from his tangled harness.

"Who found them?" I asked the elf in charge. Short fellow, Karl—but then all of the elves were—with the hairless face of a baby and shoes that curled in on themselves near the toes. Snowshoes would have been more practical, but try telling any one of them that.

Karl jingled in response. I don't mean his clothing either. His entire person resonated like a quiet, tinkling bell. It's how the elves communicate with one another, and with Nick. Don't ask me how.

I checked the elf with a look best described as impatient—or if I was forty-some years younger, sassy. "Now you know I didn't understand any of that," I said. "Let's have it the usual way."

"Usual for who?" Karl crossed his arms. He sounded like what my house cat might if she suddenly gained a voice: high, scratchy, and mildly inconvenienced. "Ivo discovered them after sunrise. We'd just finished harnessing the team."

Ivo, good. Poor elf was probably traumatized, but selfish as it was, I was relieved to learn it hadn't been Nick. He was a sensitive soul, and loved these animals to distraction. The last time one had gotten sick—Comet, I think, or maybe Cupid—he'd marched through heavy snowfall to the barn every night, comforting the reindeer with stories as if it understood him. Almost came down with something himself from all the worry. Probably would have too, had I not stopped in to check on him from time to time, making sure he ate decently and slept. Man was a workaholic. I could respect it, to a point.

I hunched down, holding my old back in place, and followed the team's tuglines with my gloved hands to the spot they terminated—a tumble of snow and blood. Beast must have dragged Dasher and Dancer off, unlucky bastards. The swing deer hadn't fared any better, though their leftover haunches and spilled intestines would give me a better idea of what I was up against.

"Where were you headed?" I asked, glancing back at the sleigh, laden with supplies.

"North," Karl said. "The big man's scouting new locations for his workshop, and wanted to leave as early as possible."

My heart stopped. *Nick's leaving?*

The possibility of losing my only friend in a hundred miles made me suddenly feel my age, but I pushed the concern aside for the moment. "Why wasn't anyone watching the team? Don't think I minced words the last time I was here."

The earthquake back in March had pushed many predators inland, and woken others who should have still been deep in hibernation. I'd had a busy spring. When Nick told me about the tracks he'd been finding in and around the barn, I warned him in no uncertain terms that he needed to keep his animals under close supervision at all times. *No going out after dark,* I'd told him while he rooted through a cabinet for marshmallows to complete our cocoa, humming a friendly tune, *and for heaven's sake, send for me if something starts to feel wrong.* I thought I'd been clear.

"Someone was *supposed* to be," Karl said.

The elves all turned to look at one of their brethren.

The elf in question wore a bright blue coat two sizes too big for him, fat mittens designed to look like kittens, complete with whiskers, and the point of his left ear was missing, the flesh folded over on itself. My business was beasts—snow chorts, akhluts, even the occasional yeti. I didn't know enough about elven physiology to be able to say with any definitiveness whether a stunted ear was a common birth defect for their kind, but to me it looked more like the result of an accident. Or an attack. Even standing in a circle of his own kind, this one seemed skittish.

"I wasn't gone for more than a few minutes," the accused elf said, shrinking in his coat.

"Tell her what you were doing, Ollie," Karl said.

"Do I have to?"

"He was inside huffing woodsmoke like some kitchen brownie."

Ollie frowned. "It sounds worse when you say it like that. I was *cold.* I'd been outside all morning, and I just wanted—"

I held up a hand. "None of that matters now. See those deep gashes on the hind leg there?" The elves turned to look. "Those were made by something big and hungry. We're dealing with an apex predator. Top of the food chain. And those sets of tracks leading away?"

The elves' heads swung the other way.

"My guess, they weren't all made by the same creature. Plenty of beasts around here capable of taking on a reindeer, but only one I know of hunts as a group. And they wouldn't have been discouraged by one little elf, I'll tell you what. Slacking off probably saved your life, Ollie."

Ollie shouted something about being a hard worker and powerfully magic, but I ignored his protest, and let my gaze move past him to the house. *Workshop.* Whatever Nick was calling it these days. A weak ribbon of smoke rose from the chimney, and the house was dark save for a single lit window on the second floor. "I told that man he needed to invest in some dogs," I muttered to myself. "Big ones."

Karl puffed himself up. "Excuse me, Miss Myra. You might know monsters, but we know how to protect our home." The other elves jingled and jangled in a chorus of agreement.

I gestured to the reindeer. "Yep. Doing a great job."

In my big ole snow boots, armed with my typical bolt-action, a couple of knives, and a slightly grumpier attitude than normal, I trudged toward Nick's place. I regretted my unkindness almost immediately, but those elves needed a wake-up call or the next time I came out here, the bodies would be considerably smaller in size. If anything was left at all.

Nick answered on the fourth knock. I heard his heavy footfalls long before the door finally creaked opened. "Thanks for coming, Myra."

I'd been prepared to give him hell for not heeding my advice, for waiting so long to ask for help when it was obvious he needed a professional, but his haggard expression postponed any lecture I might have had in mind. Plus, Nick was still in his pajamas. Good rule of thumb: if a man's in full pajamas after noon, you better believe he's having a rough day already.

"Sorry about the deer, Nick," I mumbled.

To that he said nothing. Merely nodded, scratched at his budding white beard—what I had affectionately termed his "winter coat"— and took a long breath that inflated his barrel chest like a balloon. Gesturing me inside, he showed me upstairs and into his private study, ducking beneath the doorframe which was made to fit a man half his size.

Now I've seen other men in Nick's line of work fully embrace the Thomas Nast look, bulging belly and all, but Nick wasn't fat. He was just big, which further impressed me since he had such a gentle way with the world and with everyone and everything in it. You haven't seen anything until you've seen a man with hands the size of boxer's gloves bent over a dollhouse, painting in crown molding with a fine point brush.

In that spirit, Nick's study was littered with the usual odds and ends one would expect of a toymaker's den. There were his tools, of course: a magnifying glass to help him with some of the finer details during production, glue, nuts and bolts, and countless playthings in various states of completion. I found a mobile hanging near his desk he must have been working on before I interrupted. It still smelled strongly of fresh paint, clearing my sinuses of odors best left undescribed.

Unable to help myself, I reached out to touch one of the rocket-shaped woodcuts, causing the whole apparatus to begin spinning to the tune of 'Rock-a-bye Baby'.

My throat tightened unexpectedly. Time had eliminated the possibility, but not the desire for children. Part of making my peace involved doing my job right. Even if I couldn't bring my own little squirts into the world, least I could do was look out for the ones already here.

"Do you like it?" Nick asked me, hopeful.

I was flattered my opinion mattered so much to him. "It's beautiful work," I said. An understatement, but it was what it was.

"Thank you. I had a letter from a little girl in Fairbanks the other day. Her baby brother is afraid of the dark, and all she wants for Christmas is something to ease him through the night. Isn't that wonderful?" Nick smiled, coming back into his jolly old self for a moment. I hated that I was going to be the one to bring him down again.

"That's a sweet story, Nick. But we need to talk about how we're going to solve your waheela problem."

"Waheela?"

"Bear-dogs. They hunt in groups of two or three, normally keep to the forests."

Nick looked out the window as if to assure himself that yes, we were no where near the forest.

"Normally doesn't mean always," I added. "A lot's changed since the quake."

"All right, then." Nick went and settled himself in a plush red chair whose worn cushions looked like they were in dire need of reupholstering. He tried to get me to take a seat in its twin, but I declined. I didn't plan to stay long, but I thought it might help to wait until the waheela were full, their bloodlust somewhat abated. "Tell me. What are our options?"

"Meal like the one this morning should satisfy them for the next few days, at the least." Nick blanched at the word *meal*. I pressed on, feeling awkward. Normally I didn't care how my words landed—facts were facts—but with Nick it was different. I wanted to shield him from any ugliness. "I'll track them, wait until they're asleep, and then…"

"Absolutely not," Nick cut in.

I made a face. "They slaughtered your deer."

"I won't respond to one wrong with another. My answer is no, Myra." His soft blue eyes were hard, the set of his mouth firm. "What else can we do?"

"They could have killed one of your elves," I persisted.

"Myra."

How did he not understand the danger? "The waheela hunted successfully here. Above all, they remember food, especially when it's scarce. They'll come back. You won't be safe."

Nick grew quiet. His bushy eyebrows knitted together and he laced his fingers in front of his lips, considering. In the silence I could hear the elves outside, communicating with one another in frantic tones. Sounded a lot like bickering.

"I'd hoped to wait until I had the right spot picked out, but maybe it'll have to happen sooner," Nick finally said, more to himself, it seemed, than me.

"This have anything to do with the trip you were supposed to go on this morning?"

"Karl told you."

"He mentioned it. Why haven't you?" It came out an accusation, harsher than I intended. I felt downright spiky today. Odd, since hunts usually cheered me.

Nick's face crumpled. I couldn't tell whether it was guilt or… something else.

Slowly, he rose from his chair and came toward me. I stood there in the middle of his beautiful study, chunks of ice from my boots turning to puddles on his nice hardwood floor.

"I wanted to have everything in order before I brought it up," he said.

Although he towered over me, I didn't feel intimidated. Nick radiated warmth, comfort, all the things that didn't come easily to my rough and tumble lifestyle.

And he's leaving.

"You're not happy here?" I said.

"This was never supposed to be the permanent location of my workshop. It was convenient. The Santa before me kept the buildings here in good order, but the population of Alaska has grown since his day. Now with a few of the Canadian Santas retiring, I'll have more children than ever to look after." His cheeks became a pair of small roses above the snowy timberline of his beard. "There were other reasons I've stayed as long as I have."

He stared at me until I grew self-conscious, worrying I'd smeared blood on my cheek. Wouldn't have been the first time, but it certainly wasn't a good look so near the incident with his beloved deer. I dashed my cheek, just in case.

Clearing his throat, Nick added, "Plus, you said it yourself. It's not safe here."

I straightened, latching onto those words like a drowning woman. "I can make it safe."

"You could, I don't disagree. For a time. But we both know that if it wasn't bear-dogs, it'd just be something else. Remember the ice salamander from last year?"

Of course I remembered. I'd nearly gotten myself killed after mistaking the location of its nest and running straight into the beast directly. Suffered serious frostbite for my trouble, and banged up my knee pretty bad. "I'm old," I grunted. "Not forgetful. If you think raising that old ghost is going to scare me off, you don't know me as well as I thought. I took care of the salamander, just like I'll take care of these damn waheela."

I swiveled on my heel—which admittedly wasn't great for my aforementioned knee—and made for the door. Nick clomped after me.

"Myra, wait."

"Never been much good at that," I said without stopping or turning around.

Hunting. Fighting. Scowling. Those I was good at, according to most, and it was time to put them to use. Nick was packing up and shipping out—no changing that fact. But maybe if I made him feel safe in his own home, he wouldn't feel pressured to move so soon. It would give us a little more time together.

Even if it didn't, I couldn't allow those beasts to continue as they were. The waheela were a threat to every spirited child who wandered too far from their doorstep, the explorers and the trailblazers. Nick's children. *My* children.

I had to put the waheela down.

I tracked the beasts to their den in the nearby mountains, first following the trail of blood and when that let up, the deep gouges in the snow where their paws had pressed. And where bodies had been dragged.

Along the way I discovered Dasher. Well, Dasher's *head*.

It was a fair size—about the size of a horse, maybe bigger—and yet the large reindeer had apparently presented no problem for the waheela. Doubtless they'd make quick work of me if I wasn't careful.

The reindeer's antlers had become serrated like a knife, gnawed jagged and sharp by the bear-dogs' teeth. Tendons still stood out in Dasher's neck, paused in strain, capturing his last moments as he tried to escape. I documented the damage almost clinically, as if I had never known this beautiful animal when he was alive, dancing in the sleigh line, huffing warm carrot-breath into my face. As if I had never tried feeding him his favorite snack, only to have my hand come back covered in slobber. I'd never seen Nick laugh so hard.

"Dammit," I grunted. Beating my hands against my pants, I picked myself up, and moved on.

By the time I arrived at the den, the sky was blushing red between roughened tree spines, and I knew I only had a few hours at most 'til sundown. After dark the beasts would have the advantage, not only because of lower temperatures but because my eyesight is jack shit at night.

I approached the cave where I was sure the beasts were hiding, listening for any sign of their presence. It was quiet as a held breath. Despite my best efforts to move stealthily across the rocky terrain, my own footsteps sounded loud against the silence.

Nothing suggested anyone was home, but I wasn't born yesterday. Where there wasn't blood or bone, broken branches and disturbed snow marked the narrow path the beasts had taken through the wilderness. I'd also noticed clumps of fur caught by the surrounding brush, and not all of it belonged to the waheela.

When I finally got up the courage to peer inside the cave, the beasts saw me before I saw them. Large, hulking shadows flexed within the dark—coming toward me fast. I barely managed to sight my rifle before the first monster charged, and my shot went painfully, embarrassingly wide.

So much for getting the drop on them.

The waheela knocked me back into the failing light, pinning me to the icy ground. Wind rippled the fur over its massive shoulders, while the last remnants of the sun sloped down its enormous snout and its nose glistened with blood. Beast must've been the size of a small pick-up truck. Damn near felt like it, too.

I wheezed, struggling to dislodge the waheela.

Its lips pulled back from its teeth in an angry wrinkle, spit hanging to its canines from its lower lips like webbing. I waited for it to growl or snarl.

Instead, the bear-dog *spoke*.

"This is your only warning." Its voice sounded like the choking engine of my Ski-doo. "Don't come back."

Having anticipated its snapping jaws, I'd maneuvered the barrel of my rifle between our faces. Now I lowered it as the waheela let up. Gasping, I continued to puff like a train struggling over a hill, and the only word I managed to squeeze out before the bear-dog, or whatever it was, gave me its back was: "Shapeshifter?"

"No," it said.

"Spirit animal? Some kind of lycanthrope?"

"Go away."

I'd managed to gain my feet, and with the indignant tone of a grandmother facing down a stubborn toddler said, "Then what, in god's name, *are* you?"

"All he knows," it answered, and slipped back into the shadow of the cave.

After my encounter with the All-he-knows—stupid name, but I had to call the thing something—I stumbled home, chewing on the exchange. *Who in the world is* he *and what all does he know?*

Would've been smarter to call up my old friend Enoki and have him fly out to join me, but now that one of the beasts had shown a capacity for human speech, my conscience dug its heels in whenever I considered the possibility of exterminating the group. If Nick hated the idea of killing the bear-dogs before, he'd never forgive me for going through with the hunt once he learned what had happened. It wasn't in my nature to lie, especially not to Nick, so I needed to find another solution.

The following morning, I stopped by the house to air my troubled thoughts, but Nick was away. Karl informed me that Nick had left that morning for Juneau to deliver toys to an eight-year-old girl who doctors said wouldn't live to see next Christmas. He'd taken his old beater with the sagging roof instead of the surviving members of his team, but I doubted the little girl would mind. Still it bothered me that some of the magic would be missing from the experience.

"Would you like me to pass along a message?" the head elf asked me.

I almost didn't hear him, too distracted by the clanging of bells. It was the elves again; they were ganging up on the one with the scarred ear. I lifted my chin in the direction of the scuffle. "What's that about?"

Karl didn't even turn around to look. "Family disagreement, Miss Myra. Nothing for you to worry about."

"Things seem tense around here. Noticed it even before yesterday."

"Not everyone's happy about the idea of moving farther north. But we all want what's best for the boss, and for the children." I believed him. At least I believed he believed that. Wasn't so sure about the other elves' intentions, given how loudly they were hammering one another in their strange chiming tongue.

"Everyone still blaming that one for what happened to the team?" I asked.

"Who? Ollie?" Karl shrugged. "Maybe, but that's not what they're fighting about."

"Thought we were calling it a 'family disagreement.'"

The head elf frowned, but his baby face turned it into more of a pout. "I don't know why I'm telling you any of this."

"Because I'm the only straight-shooter around these parts. Face it, you like me." I winked.

"Eh…" Karl said, slouching in a grudging way. "I've met humans I liked less."

That put a smile on this old face. I was about to leave then, but something still niggled at me. "You never said what the fight's about."

Karl screwed his mouth to one side, as if trying to decide whether to let me in on the drama. Ultimately he couldn't help himself. Elves love to gossip. "There's been talk of someone using up our magic allowance, far exceeding what any individual elf should use."

"Sorry—magic allowance?"

"*Hey*! Knock it off!" Karl snapped at the group squabbling behind him. His plain voice cut through the aggressive tinkling, and then he addressed me again in a calmer tone. "The allowance is where we get our magic from to perform all the tasks a Santa might need of us. Elves aren't magical by nature. It comes to us from the boss, who draws from the Belief—uh, the power of belief, that is—and then divvies out a reasonable portion every month. You didn't know that?"

"Still learning new things every day," I said. So Nick was magic, too. Always suspected, but it was nice to have it confirmed. "Well. Best of luck sorting out the allowance issue."

Karl saluted me. "Best of luck not getting eaten by bear-dogs."

Against the warning I'd received—and despite my better judgment— I went back to the den the next day. Only this time I went equipped with some of my big guns.

Not literal guns, mind you. I'd taken a risk and decided to leave my rifle at home, hoping it would serve as a sign of my good intentions as I crunched toward the cavemouth. Instead, I came with the best diagnostic equipment I had on hand, usually reserved for the victims of a supernatural attack, not its perpetrators. Had a feeling I might be dealing with a curse, but I wouldn't know for sure until I dangled my whalebone amulet in front of one of the creatures and saw its reaction. I had a few other tricks I could try if that failed, such as the secret songs my mother taught me as a girl to absolve transgressions, but I doubted they'd work on the All-he-knows. In any case, my gut told me I wouldn't need them.

Rather than make the same mistake I did last time and enter uninvited, I stood in the sun a fair distance away and whistled a couple times. *Here, doggy, doggy…*

One of the beasts appeared and lumbered down the hillside toward me, while behind them two pairs of reflective eyes opened in the dark. I was surprised I could see them at all, given how far back they stood, but I chalked that up to magic. A lot of magical creatures had glowing eyes. Wasn't anything to write home about, nor did it prove or disprove my theory of the presence of a curse.

"You don't listen very well," the beast said in its mangled voice.

Again I was taken aback by the sheer size of the All-he-knows. With its mass of fur and shifting muscle, it looked capable of going a round with an akhlut (though I'd still have placed money on the orca spirit).

My legs jellied, but I held my ground, clutching the amulet in my hand.

"I have something for you," I said.

"I'm going to eat you if you don't leave," the All-he-knows said.

"Don't be rude. Come here."

To my surprise—and relief—the All-he-knows came. Didn't look happy about it, judging by its narrowed eyes, but I was here to solve a problem, not make friends. Contrary to its threat, the creature didn't once try to nip me as I brought the amulet out.

Good doggy.

As soon as I held the amulet up, the All-he-knows reared, snarling, the cleansing magic doing exactly what I'd hoped. At the same time, its face seemed to—*flicker*. In the space of a single breath, I glimpsed a young girl inside the beast: frightened green eyes layered underneath its bright brown ones, a wobbling mouth behind a giant, toothy grimace.

I was right. This *was* a curse.

"What did you do?" the All-he-knows demanded, still with the same voice as before, but now I thought I heard the plaintive whine of a scared little girl underneath the deeper tones. "That hurt."

Shoving the amulet back into my pocket, I said, "How did this happen to you?"

She looked away, hanging her big head dolefully. The other cursed children slowly crept into the light, posturing in their big bear-dog bodies, as if I didn't know what they truly were. "We're not supposed to talk about it. We'll be punished more if we do. All he knows. Ask *him*."

"Who? You have to give me a name, sweetheart."

"All he."

My hand met my forehead so fast, I was surprised it didn't leave a mark. I knew I'd be needing a hearing aid some time in the near future, but this convinced me of my pressing need for one now. She hadn't been telling me an answer before, but giving me an important clue.

Ollie knows.

Whiskered mittens slapped at my arms as I hoisted twenty-five pounds of elf into the air. Ollie nearly slipped out of his puffy coat, but I trapped each of his arms in their sleeves and held fast. While I suspected the elf was using all his allowance to keep the children as animals, I knew there was still a chance he might've been able to use magic. I wore the amulet around my neck, trusting that it would protect me well enough, if that were the case.

"*What did you do to those poor children?*" I thundered.

Ollie trembled as if I were a fearsome thing, which would have pleased me in my youth. Back then, I often got labeled "cute" due to my short stature and because people didn't seem to know how else to describe a chubby, Inuit girl. I'd been glad when my hair grayed and the wrinkles came in as it finally put an end to all that nonsense. These days I liked to think I presented a visage closer to a patrician matriarch on the squat side.

"I was trying to help!" Ollie protested. "Let me down!"

"Help? Is that what you call cursing three innocent children and making them kill?"

"Let me down *or else!*" The elf continued to squirm.

"Do you even care about the damage you've caused? Nick's reindeer—"

"I had no choice. The boss left me *no choice*. He was thinking about staying here. It would have crippled operations; we don't have what we need here to expand. Not to mention the trouble with the monsters in this area. I needed to make him and the rest of the elves who were on his side see how dangerous it was."

"Those animals trusted you," I said.

Ollie had the decency to look ashamed. He blushed from his cheeks to the tip of his only pointed ear. "They weren't supposed to kill them," he whispered.

"What on earth is going on out here?"

Nick filled the open doorway of the house, looking down at us from beneath heavy white brows. He was in a red long-sleeve shirt with jeans, the closest thing he'd wear to his famous red suit until after Thanksgiving. The ensemble immediately reminded me of a conversation we'd had recently. *Maybe I'll start wearing red, too*, I told him. He smiled earnestly. *Is that so? Yes*, I replied, *it'll hide the blood.* His smile became brittle after that, until it had disappeared entirely.

He wasn't smiling now either.

"Myra? Is there a reason you've got Ollie four feet off the ground there?"

"She's attacking me!" Ollie shouted. At the same time, I felt a sting at the base of my throat. The amulet hummed, vibrating a moment before going still. Little monster had tried throwing something ugly my way, but luckily I'd taken the precautions I had.

The way Nick was looking at me—like *I* was the bad guy here—roiled my gut. "Please put Ollie down, Myra," he said.

"Oh, fine." I set the runt down. He scrambled backward toward Nick with his face puckered, primed and ready for tears. I rolled my eyes. I'd seen better acting from the grade-schoolers who performed plays at the local schoolhouse in Selawik, and one of them always has a finger up his nose by the start of intermission.

"Why don't you tell Nick what you've done, Ollie?" I said just as Karl and several other elves emerged from inside the barn, summoned by the racket.

I expected resistance from Ollie, and prepared my own version of the story to present. Instead, Ollie took one look at his brothers, one look at Nick, and completely spilled the beans.

He revealed everything: how he'd picked a couple of children off the Naughty list and transformed them into monsters. How he'd then set them upon the reindeer, hoping to convince Nick to leave and set up shop farther north. They were supposed to injure, not kill the sleigh team, but the children's bloodlust got the better of them. Ollie also admitted to siphoning magic from the elves' small summer allowance to keep the children in their cursed state so they couldn't tell anyone what had happened.

The whole time Nick listened with an inscrutable expression, saying nothing.

"I was trying to help," Ollie repeated, sobbing into Nick's pantleg. These waterworks were slightly more convincing, and despite my determination to remain hard and angry, the sight of the little elf crying tugged at my stiff heart. I didn't want to feel sympathy for the being who had caused so much needless pain and suffering, but I did.

"Sorry, boss."

After a few seconds, Nick knelt down and laid his large hand on Ollie's trembling head. The elf immediately stilled. "You made a mistake," Nick said, without anger or judgment. "We all make them. But now you must fix it."

That's it? I thought, stunned. *No condemnation? No punishment? Just... forgiveness?*

Ollie nodded. "I'll release the children from the spell."

"And see them safely back to their families. They must be worried sick and missing them."

Karl escorted Ollie away, and the other elves went back to work, leaving Nick and me alone. We stood on the porch of the house, shaded by the overhang. I rested my hands on the railing, then Nick rested his beside mine, our pinkies just touching. It was such a sweet, innocent effort that I had to laugh.

"You make me feel like a girl sometimes," I confessed.

"I hope that's a good thing," Nick said, smiling.

"It's certainly something." I looked out toward the barn, heavy. "Ollie did serious harm this week, and he could've done worse."

"Yes."

"Is that all you're going to say? What if he tries to pull another stunt like this?"

Nick picked at his beard. "Oh, I'm not too concerned. I imagine the elves will find a way to punish Ollie appropriately. They like to keep the discipline in-house. And Ollie seems sorry. I doubt he'll ever try anything of the sort again."

"He seems sorry? I could have killed those kids, Nick," I whispered, my voice husky with emotion. Tried clearing my throat, but it didn't help. "Maybe I'm getting too old for this."

"Now I doubt that. But maybe it is time for a change."

Nick folded his hand over mine, sending a shot of warmth through the rest of my body like a jolt of caffeine. The gesture pulled my eyes to his.

"Ollie had good reason to be concerned about me staying," he said. "After all, you're here."

"Me?" I blurted. "Don't you put your indecision on me, Mister Claus."

"No, no. It isn't like that. I've stayed because I hoped you and I… well." I wasn't some ingénue; I knew full well what he was trying to say, but I wanted him to *actually say it*. "You are a remarkable woman. Tough as nails, but caring too. I know you look out for me, but I've also seen how you watch over everyone in these parts. Your friendship, wisdom, and strength have all been a great source of comfort to me over the years, and I always value our time together."

A smile pulled at my lips. "I feel the same, Nick."

"The last time we spoke, I wanted to ask you something. I don't need your answer right this moment, but if you would just consider the possibility…"

"Say your piece already, you old codger."

"I'd like you to come with me. To the North Pole."

While he waited for my reply, he knocked his boots on the porch—big black boots remarkably like the pair I often trudged around in. We were rubbing off on one another, ole Nick and I. Given a couple more years, I suspected we'd be distinguishable as a couple on sight. Rather than repulse, the thought filled me with a peculiar glee.

"What am I going to do in the North Pole?" I asked, trying to be realistic. "Make toys?"

Nick grabbed his stomach, laughing. "I'd like to see the toys you'd make! Guns and traps and shiny little amulets to ward off evil. No, I don't imagine you'd make toys, though I'm sure there are children out there much like yourself when you were their age who would enjoy them."

"I'm not cut out for housework. Barely manage to keep my own shack free of cobwebs."

"I'm not looking for a maid, Myra. I want a companion. A

partner. Someone to keep me sharp and honest. Who loves protecting children as much as I do. Who will tell me how it is, and make sure the elves don't get out of line." Smiling again, he turned and I turned with him, my hands still wrapped in his like a gift. "And who knows? Maybe you'll find a beast or two to hunt up there in the wild north. You do whatever makes you happiest."

Hunting had always supplied me with purpose, a constant reason to get up in the morning, but I wasn't sure it made me happy anymore, not like when I was young and eager to strut my stuff. The corpse of a preternatural creature didn't warm an old woman's bones at night (well, unless you set it on fire, but then there was the smell to deal with...).

At the end of the day, adventure made me happiest. Moving north with Nick seemed like it would be a good one.

I gave him a sly look. "I expect you'll be wanting to marry me at some point."

"The thought had crossed my mind. 'Missus Claus, Monster Hunter.' It'll be good for a few new songs, I think."

I chuckled. "All right, but I get to pick the animals for the team. Reindeer are far too temperamental. You'd be better off with—"

"Dogs, I know. But who ever heard of a team of flying dogs?"

"I was going to say polar bears."

"Polar bears!"

"You'd rather have narwhals?"

We bantered long into the evening, first over a hearty dinner of lamb chops and potatoes and on through hot chocolate afterward. As the fire wore down in the giant hearth in the front room, we moved upstairs to warmer climes.

Outside the wind howled like a demon, scraping at the roof. When my heart settled down long enough for me to hear it, I briefly thought of the reindeer tucked away in Nick's barn, snug in their beds of warm hay. Maybe they dreamt of the monsters who'd claimed their brothers. Maybe they dreamt nothing at all. Either way they were survivors who deserved old age and the happiness that a lucky few find during it.

"Maybe we'll keep the deer," I said into Nick's shoulder.

And so we did.

ABOUT THE AUTHORS

Laura VanArendonk Baugh writes speculative fiction in several flavors as well as non-fiction which manages not to be boring. She frequently draws on mythological and folkloric sources. Her Norse mythology novel *The Songweaver's Vow* is a semi-finalist for the SPF Best of 2017. Find her at www.LauraVAB.com.

C.B. Calsing is a writer, editor, and educator living on the Island of Hawaii. She graduated from the Creative Writing Workshop at the University of New Orleans. Learn more at cbcalsing.blogspot.com.

DJ Tyrer is the person behind *Atlantean Publishing*, was short-listed for the 2015 Carillon 'Let's Be Absurd' Fiction Competition, and has been widely published in anthologies and magazines around the world, such as *Warlords of the Asteroid Belt* (Rogue Planet Press), *Strangely Funny II, III, and IV* (all Mystery & Horror LLC), *Steam Chronicles* (Zimbell House) and *Irrational Fears* (FTB Press), and issues of *Tigershark* and *Sirens Call*, and also has a novella available in paperback and on the Kindle, *The Yellow House* (Dunhams Manor).

DJ Tyrer's website is at djtyrer.blogspot.co.uk

The Atlantean Publishing website is at: atlanteanpublishing.blogspot.co.uk

Jennifer Lee Rossman is a science fiction geek from Oneonta, New York, where she cross stitches and threatens to run over people with her wheelchair. Her work has been featured in *Circuits & Slippers, Expanded Horizons,* and *Cast of Wonders.* You can find her blog at jenniferleerossman.blogspot.com and Twitter at twitter.com/JenLRossman

Kristen Lee is a senior at Kendall College of Art and Design who picked up writing and ran with it. She enjoys tea, blue ink pens, and Oxford commas. She resides in Grand Rapids, Michigan with her cat.

Randi Perrin has spent her entire life writing in one form or another. In fact, if she wasn't writing, she'd likely go completely and utterly insane. Her husband has learned to recognize when the voices are talking in her head and she needs some quality time with an empty Word file (the key to a successful marriage with a writer). A pop-culture junkie, she has been known to have entire conversations in movie quotes and/or song lyrics.

She is the author of the Earthbound Angels trilogy, the contemporary romance novella, *Anticipating Temptation*, and several of her short stories have appeared in anthologies.

Michael Leonberger is a writer and teacher from Virginia, where he lives with his girlfriend and their pet turtle, Tippy.

His writing credits include a novel (*Halloween Sweets*), several short stories, annual contributions to the online journal *Digital America*, various screenplays (most notably *Goodish*, an official selection at the 2014 Virginia Film Festival in Charlottesville, VA), and a macabre series of poetry called *Death Haikus*, illustrated by his girlfriend for Nun Comix.

His work tends to fall somewhere between horror and comedy, with a body of work that focuses on anxiety, guilt, and the inevitable scarring that comes from survival.

Andrew Wilson is a fantasy and science fiction author from northern California.

Ross Van Dusen has won two Clio Awards, an International Broadcasting Award, British International Award, multiple ADDY, ANDY, and Belding awards. When he retired as Executive Vice

President, Creative Director of Chiat/Day Advertising in San Francisco, he turned to art and writing.

He's had fine art shows throughout the US. He's written and published ten light-hearted mysteries for adults.

His five children's books have won thirteen awards, including Gold in the 2016 Moonbeam Children's Book Awards.

Ross has two grown children, one grandchild, and two great grandchildren. He lives with his wife, Jean, and her cat, in Albuquerque, New Mexico.

M. L. D. Curelas lives in Calgary, Canada, with two humans and a varying number of guinea pigs. Raised on a diet of Victorian literature and Stephen King, it's unsurprising that she now writes and edits fantasy and science fiction. Her most recent short fiction can be found in the anthologies *Equus; Brave New Girls: Stories of Girls Who Science and Scheme;* and *49th Parallels.* Margaret is also the owner of Tyche Books, a Canadian small press which publishes science fiction and fantasy.

Maren Matthias currently lives in Chicago, where she operates as an actor, cat-whisperer, and wannabe-pirate. She loves airports with the adventures they promise and spends her spare time sword-fighting with friends in their backyards. She was last published by Transmundane Press and is thrilled to be a part of this anthology.

Anne Luebke has a degree in Biochemistry and currently works for the Gene Expression Center at UW-Madison. She spends most of her working hours moving small bits of water from one place to another, which gives her plenty of time to think up fantastic stories but very little time to write them down.

Jeff Kuykendall's speculative fiction has appeared in *Whiteside Review, The Singularity,* and *Fiction Vortex.* He blogs weekly about cult cinema at MidnightOnly.com. Jeff earned an MFA from the University of Washington and is a veteran of the Madison Writers' Studio in Madison, Wisconsin. He's a former award recipient for short fiction in the National Foundation for Advancement in the Arts' Arts Recognition and Talent Search, and currently lives in southwestern Wisconsin.

Hayley Stone is a writer, editor, and poet from California. Her debut sci-fi novel, *Machinations*, was chosen as an Amazon Best Sci-fi & Fantasy Book of the Year for 2016. When not reading or writing, Hayley studies history, falls in love with video game characters, and analyzes buildings for velociraptor entry points. Find her at www.hnstoneauthor.com and on Twitter @hayley_stone.

ABOUT THE ANTHOLOGIST

Rhonda Parrish is driven by a desire to do All. The. Things. She is an Assistant Editor at World Weaver Press, edits anthologies (most recently this one!), co-wrote a paranormal non-fiction title, *Haunted Hospitals*, and has had her shorter works included in dozens of publications including *Tesseracts 17* and *Imaginarium: The Best Canadian Speculative Writing* (2012 & 2015).

Her website is www.rhondaparrish.com

Thank you for reading!

We hope you'll leave an honest review at Amazon, Goodreads, or wherever you discuss books online.

Leaving a review means a lot for the authors and editors who worked so hard to create this book.

Please sign up for our newsletter for news about upcoming titles, submission opportunities, special discounts, & more.

WorldWeaverPress.com/newsletter-signup

HE SEES YOU WHEN HE'S CREEPIN': TALES OF KRAMPUS
Edited by Kate Wolford

Krampus is the cloven-hoofed, curly-horned, and long-tongued dark companion of St. Nick. Sometimes a hero, sometimes a villain, within these pages, he's always more than just a sidekick. You'll meet manifestations of Santa's dark servant as he goes toe-to-toe with a bratty Cinderella, a guitar-slinging girl hero, a coffee shop-owning hipster, and sometimes even St. Nick himself. Whether you want a dash of horror or a hint of joy and redemption, these 12 new tales of Krampus will help you gear up for the most "wonderful" time of the year.

Featuring original stories by Steven Grimm, Lissa Marie Redmond, Beth Mann, Anya J. Davis, E.J. Hagadorn, S.E. Foley, Brad P. Christy, Ross Baxter, Nancy Brewka-Clark, Tamsin Showbrook, E.M. Eastick, and Jude Tulli.

"While some of these stories might be a little more dark or cynical than typical holiday fare (which might be a perk for some people tired of extra cheesy Christmas entertainment), not only are they thought provoking, but they retain a sense of the wonder and magic of Christmas."
—*Tales of Faerie*

"These stories were well chosen, and this anthology is perfect for those of you that like Nightmare Before Christmas and other Halloween/Christmas crosses. This one is worth checking out if you like unique and interesting stories."
—*Hollie Ohs Book Reviews*

KRAMPUSNACHT: TWELVE NIGHTS OF KRAMPUS
A Christmas Krampus anthology
Edited by Kate Wolford

For bad children, a lump of coal from Santa is positively light punishment when Krampus is ready and waiting to beat them with a stick, wrap them in chains, and drag them down to hell—all with St. Nick's encouragement and approval.

Krampusnacht holds within its pages twelve tales of Krampus triumphant, usurped, befriended, and much more. From evil children (and adults) who get their due, to those who pull one over on the ancient "Christmas Devil." From historic Europe, to the North Pole, to present day American suburbia, these all new stories embark on a revitalization of the Krampus tradition.

Whether you choose to read *Krampusnacht* over twelve dark and scary nights or devour it in one *nacht* of joy and terror, these stories are sure to add chills and magic to any winter's reading.

Featuring original stories by Elizabeth Twist, Elise Forier Edie, Jill Corddry, Colleen H. Robbins, Caren Gussoff, Lissa Sloan, Patrick Evans, Guy Burtenshaw, Jeff Provine, Mark Mills, Cheresse Burke, and Scott Farrell.

"A kaleidoscope of Krampus tales featuring enjoyable twists and turns. Imaginative and entertaining."
— Monte Beauchamp, Krampus: The Devil of Christmas

"From funny to pure terror. The writers also tell us their inspiration for each story which helps put us in the right frame of mind. I really enjoyed all these tales, and it was a great introduction to Krampus for me. I like that he is about justice, not just doing harm for the sake of evil. What makes it even better is that he has Santa's blessing. **This is a must-read for the upcoming holiday season.**"
— *Bitten By Books*

FROZEN FAIRY TALES
Edited By Kate Wolford

Winter is not coming. Winter is here.

As unique and beautifully formed as a snowflake, each of these fifteen stories spins a brand new tale or offers a fresh take on an old favorite like Jack Frost, The Snow Queen, or The Frog King. From a drafty castle to a blustery Japanese village, from a snow-packed road to the cozy hearth of a farmhouse, from an empty coffee house in Buffalo, New York, to a cold night outside a university library, these stories fully explore the perils and possibilities of the snow, wind, ice, and bone-chilling cold that traditional fairy tale characters seldom encounter.

In the bleak midwinter, heed the irresistible call of fairy tales. Just open these pages, snuggle down, and wait for an icy blast of fantasy to carry you away. With all new stories of love, adventure, sorrow, and triumph by Tina Anton, Amanda Bergloff, Gavin Bradley, L.A. Christensen, Steven Grimm, Christina Ruth Johnson, Rowan Lindstrom, Alison McBain, Aimee Ogden, J. Patrick Pazdziora, Lissa Marie Redmond, Anna Salonen, Lissa Sloan, Charity Tahmaseb, and David Turnbull to help you dream through the cold days and nights of this most dreaded season.

THE NAUGHTY LIST
Red Moon Anthologies, Volume Two
Edited by Cori Vidae

Six holiday romances, from sexy to sweet, prove love is better on the Naughty List. Featuring stories by Tiffany Reisz, Alexa Piper, Pumpkin Spice, Elizabeth Black, Doug Blakeslee, and Wendy Sparrow.

"Warm and spicy as mulled wine, rich and decadent as eggnog, the perfect holiday read for snuggling up by the fire!"
— Christine Morgan, author of *Murder Girls*

World Weaver Press, LLC
Publishing fantasy, paranormal, and science fiction.
We believe in great storytelling.
WorldWeaverPress.com

Made in the USA
San Bernardino, CA
09 November 2017